Other Harold Courlander Books from Henry Holt

THE AFRICAN

THE COW-TAIL SWITCH
and Other West African Stories

THE FIRE ON THE MOUNTAIN
and Other Stories from Ethiopia and Eritrea

THE TIGER'S WHISKER
and Other Tales from Asia and the Pacific

PEOPLE OF THE SHORT BLUE CORN

HAROLD COURLANDER

PEOPLE OF THE SHORT BLUE CORN

TALES AND LEGENDS OF THE HOPI INDIANS

❖

ILLUSTRATED BY
ENRICO ARNO

HENRY HOLT AND COMPANY ❖ NEW YORK

Henry Holt and Company, Inc.
Publishers since 1866
115 West 18th Street
New York, New York 10011

Henry Holt is a registered trademark of Henry Holt and Company, Inc.

Published in Canada by Fitzhenry & Whiteside Ltd.,
195 Allstate Parkway, Markham, Ontario L3R 4T8.

Library of Congress Cataloging-in-Publication Data
Courlander, Harold. People of the short blue corn: tales and legends
of the Hopi Indians / Harold Courlander; illustrated by Enrico Arno.
        p.   cm.
Originally published: New York: Harcourt Brace Jovanovich, 1970.
Summary: A collection of seventeen traditional tales from the Hopi.
1. Hopi Indians—Folklore.   2. Tales—Arizona.   [1. Hopi Indians—
    Folklore.   2. Indians of North America—Arizona—Folklore.
      3. Folklore—Arizona.]   I. Arno, Enrico, ill.   II. Title.
    E99.H7C65   1996   398.2'089974—dc20   95-37318

ISBN 0-8050-3511-7

Cover illustration by John Hart

First published in hardcover in 1970 by Harcourt Brace Jovanovich, Inc.
First Owlet edition published in 1996 by Henry Holt and Company, Inc.
Printed in the United States of America on acid-free paper. ∞
            1   3   5   7   9   10   8   6   4   2

Contents

❖

PEOPLE OF THE SHORT BLUE CORN

The Land of
the Hopis

❖

Long before Europeans came to live in the New World, the Indians who call themselves the Hopis had settled in the American Southwest, built their stone villages, cultivated the land, and given names to the mountains, rivers, hills, cliffs, springs, and mesas.

Why they chose this country cannot be easily explained, for it is a place where sometimes the rains forget to fall and the springs dry up, where winter winds can bring great blizzards that bury the land deep in snow. Probably, like other peoples who came to the New World much later, the Hopis were searching for a better life. But that does not mean an easy life. Their legends contained the prophecy that they would struggle hard with nature to fulfill their needs, and this is the way it has been in the semidesert country in which they live. Whatever the circumstances were that set them on their journeys from one place to another, they eventually found in what is now called northern Arizona a place to their liking, a place of beauty and awesome sights. And having found it, they said, "Here we will stay. Let us build our houses."

Oraibi is the oldest of the occupied Hopi villages. Six centuries ago, long before Columbus reached the New World, the Hopis were living there. They or their ancestors would have smiled to hear of the discovery of America, for they were in the land long before then and knew it to be ancient. They had already learned to grow cotton, to spin it into thread, and to weave it into cloth. They had learned how to make fine pottery and had developed a variety of maize that would grow in dry and rocky ground. And they had created a religious life that kept them in balance with the mountains, the mesas, and the deserts that surrounded them.

How many villages the Hopis and their ancestors built and lived in before they abandoned them is not known. But on the great mesa where most of the occupied villages now stand, there were once many others that today are only windswept ruins, and in all directions beyond the mesa itself lie the remains of other villages that the Hopis say were made and lived in by their people. Some of the ancient villages have names, but most are nameless. There are legends that explain why certain villages are without people. Some, it is said, were destroyed by invaders. Some were destroyed by the Hopis themselves. Others were abandoned because of misfortunes that came when the people forgot to live virtuously. And there were some that had to be left behind because of drought and the threat of famine. The legends say that some of the villages were consumed by fire, while others were washed away by flood.

Yet Oraibi remains standing there on the mesa. Some of its

stone walls have crumbled, but it is still a living village. The Hopis have survived conflicts with marauding tribes, conquest by the Spanish, and the arrival of other whites from the Atlantic side of the continent. They are there in Oraibi and the other old—even ancient—settlements built by their ancestors: Shongopovi, Mishongnovi, Shipaulovi, Walpi, Sichomovi, Hano, Moencopi, and some of more recent beginnings. The people rebuild their walls when time and weather crumble them, weave cotton and wool, and make pottery and baskets in the old patterns.

There have been changes in the Hopi country. A hard-surface road passes close to the villages, and there is also running water and electricity now. Some Hopis ride to their fields on horses or mules, but there are also pickup trucks. And a house whose foundations were built before the arrival of the first European settlers may have a television antenna on its roof.

But though many outward things have changed, the people still tell the old stories of adventure, of magic and sorcery, of courage and great deeds. They tell of men turned into animals and animals turned into men, of human wisdom and stupidity, and of the unending foolishness of the clown named Coyote. And they tell of the origin of all things, and how the Hopis left their former world below the surface of the earth to come to the place where they now live.

How the People Came from the Lower World

❖

In ancient times, the old men say, the people lived in the Lower World. Everything went well with them there. Rain was plentiful, water flowed in the springs and the streams, and corn grew plentifully in the fields. In the beginning, the tribes and the villages were at peace with one another. But somehow things changed. People began to quarrel. They no longer respected one another. They rejected the advice of their chiefs, and the chiefs became angry with the people. Sorcerers began to work evil magic that brought sickness and other misfortunes. What one person had, another person wanted. If one man spoke a thoughtful word, another man would not listen. There was bad feeling everywhere. And people became lazy. The men did not take care of their crops. The women did not make their pottery. They preferred to play games and gamble. This is the way things were. Then the streams and rivers began to dry up. The people had their kachina dances and asked for rain, but rain did not come. The corn and squash withered in the fields. And cold winds began to blow from the north.

A certain chief and the elders of his village became worried about the way things were going. They met in their kiva and talked about it. At last they made a decision. All those people who wished to continue living in this turmoil could do so. But all those who wanted a better way of life would leave. The question then was asked, "Where can we go?" It was recalled by some of the men that from time to time footsteps had been heard in the sky, as though a person were walking there. They also remembered hearing it said that somewhere above them there existed an uninhabited world. They decided to find out if this was true.

So the chief called for the men with special powers to come forward. The medicine men assembled. The chief asked them to make a bird. They shaped a bird out of clay and covered it with a woven ritual cloth called an owa. They placed their hands beneath the cloth and sang, and did with their hands what no one could see. Then they removed the owa cloth, and where there had been a piece of clay without life, there was now a living blackbird.

The blackbird asked, "Why have you called me?"

The chief answered, "We have called you so that you may find out if there is another world above us."

The blackbird said, "I shall go."

He flew into the sky. He mounted higher and higher. He became tired, but still he went upward until he saw an opening in the sky. It was like looking up through the entrance of a kiva. But the blackbird was too tired to go on, and he returned to the place where the chief and the medicine men were waiting, saying, "I went up. I found an opening there like the opening of a kiva. But my strength was gone, and I had to return."

The chief asked the medicine men to make a stronger bird. They shaped another bird out of clay and covered it with the owa cloth. They exerted their powers, and when they removed the owa, the clay bird had become a living hummingbird.

"It is small," the chief said. "How can it do what the blackbird could not do?"

But the medicine men answered, "It is a hummingbird. Though it is small, it has great strength."

Then the hummingbird spoke, saying, "Why have you called me?"

The chief instructed him to pass through the opening in the sky and find out what lay beyond. The hummingbird went up. He reached the opening in the sky and passed through it. He saw mountains and plains, but he discovered no living things, and he returned.

He said, "I flew until I was tired. Then I came back. I saw the other world. It is truly large. There are mountains, rivers, and mesas, but I saw nothing that was alive."

So the people discussed the matter. Again they recalled hearing the sound of footsteps in the sky. And they agreed that more must be known about the world above. The chief asked the medicine men to make one more bird. As before, they shaped a bird out of clay and covered it with the owa cloth. When they were finished with their work they removed the cloth and revealed a living mockingbird.

The mockingbird asked, "Why have you called me?"

The chief replied, "The blackbird could not pass through the opening in the sky. The hummingbird passed through but came back before discovering who makes the sound of walking up there. That is your task. Go there and return, and let us know what you have seen."

The mockingbird flew up. He passed through the opening in the sky. He flew far beyond where the hummingbird had gone. He reached a country of great mesas and came to a place called Ojaivi. There was a single house there, surrounded by fertile fields of corn. The mockingbird saw a person sitting in front of the house. He saw the person's face. The eyes were sunken in, and black lines were painted across the cheekbones. The mockingbird recognized him. He was Masauwu, Lord of the Upper World and Guardian of the Land of the Dead.

Masauwu said, "Welcome. I have had no visitors before. Why do you come?"

The mockingbird replied, "Down below, where the people are living, things are not good. The rain does not fall, the springs do not flow, the corn does not grow, and misfortune is everywhere. The people want to come here to the Upper World, and I have been sent to ask your permission."

Masauwu said, "There are fields here. There are springs, and the rain falls. You see how it is. If the people choose to come, let them come."

The mockingbird said, "I shall tell them what I have seen and what I have heard from your mouth."

He left Masauwu, passed again through the opening that led to the Lower World, and went down to where the people were waiting.

"I went up," he said, "and I arrived at the place of the one who lives there. He is Masauwu, Lord of the Upper World and Guardian of the Land of the Dead. He spoke to me, saying, 'There are fields. There are springs, and the rain falls. If the people choose to come, let them come.'"

So the people prepared for the journey. But they asked, "How shall we ever reach the opening in the sky?" They thought about the matter, and after they discussed it they sent for the chipmunk to help them. The chipmunk came. He planted a sunflower seed and gave the people a song to sing. They sang, and by the power that is in singing they made the sunflower grow. It grew tall, but before it reached the opening it bent over because of the weight of its blossom. Then the chipmunk planted a pine seed, and by the power of song they made it grow, but the tree was not tall enough to reach the opening. So the chipmunk planted again. This time it was a reed. By the spirit of singing they made it grow straight and tall, and it did not stop growing until it had passed through the opening in the sky.

And now Gogyeng Sowuti, Spider Grandmother, came to them. Spider Grandmother was an ancient one. She had been present on the earth since the beginning of things. Sometimes she had the form of an old woman, sometimes the form of a spider.

Spider Grandmother said, "I will climb the reed and hold it at the top so that it does not shake."

She took the form of a spider and climbed the reed. After passing through the opening, she stood at the edge and held the reed steady. The people who had chosen to leave the Lower World began to go up one at a time. The mockingbird flew up again and stood at Spider Grandmother's side. As each person came through the opening and stepped into the Upper World, the mockingbird gave him a language to speak.

"You," he said to one, "shall be a Hopi and speak the Hopi language. And you," he said to another, "shall be a Navaho and speak the Navaho language. And you," he said to another, "shall be an Apache and speak the language of the Apache."

To others he gave the languages of the Paiute, or Zuñi, or White Man. And then he explained that the tribes would disperse, each going its own way.

But people were still climbing up from below. The chief said, "All those of good heart have already arrived. The others who are following us are the troublemakers who brought misfortune to us down below. Therefore, let no one else come through."

They called down to people who were still on the way, saying, "Those of good heart have already arrived. Let no more come." But the people kept trying to come up. So the chief took hold of the reed on which they were climbing and pulled it out of the ground. He shook it, and the climbers fell back into the Lower World. Those who had already passed through the opening in the sky were the people who were to spread out and occupy the

Upper World. They made a camp nearby where they could rest and discuss matters, such as where they would go and when they would begin.

But while they were busy with these things, the chief's son became ill and died. They grieved and buried him. Afterwards they talked about it and concluded that the boy had been killed by a sorcerer who had managed to come with them from the Lower World.

The chief said, "We came here to escape from the evil people who brought misfortune on us down below. But a sorcerer is among us. Who has done this thing?" But no one spoke, and the chief went on, "Very well. We have the knowledge that will point him out." He made a ball of cornmeal. He said, "May this ball of meal fall upon the evil one," and he threw it into the air. It fell on the head of a young woman.

The chief said, "You, then, are the one."

The young woman answered, "Yes, I also have come."

The chief said, "You, who have killed my son, must return to the Lower World." He seized her to throw her back through the opening.

But she said, "Wait. It is true that I did this to your son. But he is not truly dead. He is alive down below. All who die here will return to the Lower World and live on."

The chief said, "It cannot be so. He lies buried here, where we placed him."

The young woman said, "Look through the opening. You will see your son down below."

The chief looked. He saw his son down there playing with other children. He said, "Yes, it is so. My son lives on."

The young woman said, "This is the way it will always be with us. When a person dies he will return to the other place and resume his life there. Therefore, do not send me back. Let me stay. Should things ever go badly for the people here, I will use all my powers to help them."

There was a great discussion. People said one thing and another. At last they decided. They said, "Let her stay in the Upper World. It is true that she is evil. But good and evil are everywhere. From the beginning to the end of time the two must struggle with each other. So let the woman stay. But she may not go with us. She must remain here until we are gone. After that she may go wherever she wishes." This is the way it was settled.

Now, in the Upper World things were visible, but it was not light as it is today. So the medicine men took a piece of owa cloth and cut a piece out of it in the shape of a disk. Spider Grandmother picked up the disk of cloth and went away with it to the east, and after a while they saw it rise in the sky and called it the moon. It gave a little light, but not enough, and the people said that more was needed. So the medicine men took a piece of buckskin and cut another disk from it. They painted a design on the disk and covered it with the yolks of eggs, giving it a golden color. This disk Spider Grandmother carried away, also to the east, and the people waited. Spider Grandmother placed the disk in the sky. Things became light, and warmth fell over the earth. Now the people had the sun.

When all this had been accomplished, the mockingbird said, "There is one thing more, the selection of the corn." The people gathered around the mockingbird. He placed a number of corn ears on the ground. They were of many colors. One ear was yellow, one was white, one was red, one was gray, some were speckled with different colors, and one was a short, stubby ear with blue kernels. The mockingbird said, "Each of these ears brings with it a way of life. For the one who chooses the yellow ear there will be a short life, but the years of that life will be full of enjoyment and prosperity. The short ear with the blue kernels, that is different. He who chooses it will have a life full of work and hardship, but his years will be many, and he will live into the time of his great grandchildren." The mockingbird described each ear of corn, telling of its meaning. And when he was finished he invited the people to select the ears they wanted.

Everyone considered which ears were the best. Then the Navahos reached out and took the yellow corn, which would bring a short life but much enjoyment and prosperity. Then the Sioux reached out and took the white corn. The Supais chose the ear speckled with yellow, the Comanches took the red, and the Utes chose the flint corn. Every tribe got something, all but the Hopis. And now there was only one ear left, the short blue corn. So the Hopis picked up the short blue ear, saying, "We were slow in choosing. Therefore, we must take the smallest ear of all. We shall have a life of work and hardship. But it will be a long-lasting life. Other tribes may perish, but we, the Hopis, shall survive all things." Thus the Hopis became the people of the short blue corn.

And now it was time for the journeys to start. Those who were called White Men went southward. Those who called themselves Navaho went north. The Paiutes, the Apaches, and the Zuñis, each went a different way. And this is the way the tribes dispersed over the land. As for the Hopis, they traveled eastward toward the place where Masauwu lived. The journey took many days, but when they arrived, they saw Masauwu, Lord of the Upper World and Guardian of the Land of the Dead, just as the mockingbird had described him. He had sunken eyes and wore black lines painted across his cheeks.

They said, "We are here. We received the message that we could settle in the Upper World. So we left the world down below and came through the opening in the sky. Now we have arrived."

Masauwu turned his face and looked upon them. They felt fear at first, because they saw death in his eyes. But when he spoke, it was with gentleness. He said, "Yes, I have permitted you to come. In time you will build your villages here. First, however, you must finish your migrations."

The people said, "We do not understand about the migrations."

Masauwu said, "Your journey from the Lower World was only the beginning. Now you must go to the four directions, exploring the land and learning about things. You must learn that the bear, the badger, the eagle, and all other creatures are our brothers. They are a part of our life. The rain, the corn, the sunlight, the cold wind from the north, they are all part of the heartbeat of the world. You must learn also that the earth is our mother. Out of the earth comes the water we drink and the corn that we eat. And when a man dies, the dried stalk of his body is buried, and the earth receives it. These are among the things you must discover for yourselves before you return to build your villages. The short blue corn that you have received as your portion will help to guide you."

So the Hopi people prepared for the journeys that lay ahead. Their leaders gathered to make plans. It was said, "Some of us will go one way, some will go another. So let each group have its own wanderings and be known by its own name. Let each group become a clan, and let each clan have its own mark to place upon the rocks to show that it passed by." Then the leader of one group said, "Yes, our people shall be known as the Bear Clan, for on our way to this place we discovered the carcass of a bear." Another leader said, "Yes, our group will be known as the Strap Clan, for we also saw the carcass of the bear, and from its hide we cut straps to help us carry our loads." Another said, "We shall be known as the Eagle Clan, for we saw an eagle in the sky this morning." Another said, "We shall be called the Fire Clan." Another said, "We shall be the Sun Clan, for we are the ones who decorated the sun with egg yolks before Spider Grandmother carried it into the sky." Each group claimed its name. There was the Cloud Clan, the Badger Clan, the Bow Clan, the Spruce Clan, the Coyote Clan, the Snake Clan, and many more.

When everything was ready the clans departed. Some clans went one way, some another. After they had traveled a great distance they would stop, build a village, and remain for a while. They would grow corn and do the other things they had to do. Sometimes they would remain many years at such a place. Then they would leave the village and continue their migration, just as Masauwu had instructed them to do. They left their trails on the ground, and their writings and pictures on the rocks. What they wrote was that the Bear Clan had settled here for a while and moved on, or that the Badger Clan had camped at a certain spring, or that the Corn Clan had turned here and gone in another direction.

And the short blue corn they had received from the mockingbird helped to guide them. If they planted their seed and the corn ears did not mature, then the people knew they had taken a wrong way, and they would turn back. The Bear Clan went first to the west, and then it turned north. When it arrived at a certain place, it built a village and planted. But the growing season was too short, and the corn didn't mature. So the people knew they had gone too far north, and they abandoned their village and returned southward. It went on this way. Many years passed. Many villages were built and left behind. Today the ruins of those ancient villages are still to be seen.

Then, at last, the people of the clans saw a great shower of stars fall in the night, and they knew that their migrations were over. They began the return journey.

The people of the Bear Clan were the first to return. They

arrived at a place near where the village of Shongopovi now stands. They went to Masauwu and said, "We have completed our journey. You be our chief and give us land to till."

Masauwu answered, "No, I will not be your chief. But I will give you fields where you can grow your corn and melons." He went down to where the land was fertile and stepped off the fields for the Bear Clan. He walked a great distance in one direction, then another, and finally came back to where he had started. He said, "All the lands around which I have walked are yours."

The Bear Clan people then asked, "Where shall we live?"

Masauwu replied, "Over there, to the east. Build your houses there. Your village will be called Masipa."

The people of the Bear Clan built their houses and planted their corn, and Masipa was the first village constructed by the Hopi on land given them by Masauwu. In time it came to be known as Shongopovi. Soon the other clans began to arrive, and they too were given land and a place to build. One by one other villages appeared. Some of them remain there to this day, but some are no longer there, having disappeared, just as Masauwu himself became invisible and was seen no more.

When the people of long ago came out of the Lower World, there was a sorceress among them. They had listened to her pleadings and had not sent her back because she promised to use her knowledge of magic to perform good deeds. But she forgot her promise and taught sorcery to others, until at last there were many sorcerers in the Upper World. They caused sickness and anger to go around the land. Once the Hopis and the Navahos and the Apaches were friends, but the sorcerers caused them to become enemies to one another. They also caused the White Men to return and treat the Hopis badly. Because one sorceress was allowed to come with the people from the Lower World, today there is trouble and dissension everywhere. Still, the Hopis live on where they are, for theirs is the land assigned to them in ancient days by Masauwu, Lord of the Upper World and Guardian of the Land of the Dead.

Coyote Helps
Decorate the Night

❖

In the beginning, before people came, there were only animals on the earth. It was the animals who arranged things. They all worked except Coyote. He was lazy. He merely watched. The other animals put the rivers where they are now, so that there would be water to drink. They put mountains here and there for beauty. They made trees and forests for shade. They made grass grow. They created the desert, putting down sand and all kinds of rocks, and then to make the desert attractive to look at, they painted the rocks pink and yellow and other colors. They caused cactus to grow, and put lakes in different places.

They looked at what they had done and said, "It is not enough." So they made mesas and canyons. They went on decorating the earth every way they could think of. And finally, when things were nearly finished, they did one more thing. They made hundreds and hundreds of small shiny objects with which they planned to complete their work. But they didn't know what to do with them. Some said, "Put them on the mountains." Some said, "Sprinkle them around the desert." Some said, "Hang them in the trees." They could not agree. So they left the pile of shiny objects on the ground and went home to sleep.

While they slept, Coyote came to see what they had been doing all day. He sniffed at the objects. He picked one up and examined it closely. "What is this?" he said. And seeing no use for it, he tossed it into the air. He picked up another and looked at it. "What is this good for?" he said. And he tossed it over his shoulder. Again he picked up one of the objects. "What is this supposed to be?" He threw it away in disgust. One by one he examined the shiny things, and finding them not good to eat or useful in any way, he threw them into the air, until at last they were all gone.

Then he looked up into the sky and saw them where he had thrown them, tiny spots of light in the darkness. This is how the stars came to be where they are. Coyote the busybody was responsible.

Sikakokuh and the Hunting Dog

❖

It was still the time of ancient things. When the clans had finished their migrations and began to build their villages, Gogyeng Sowuti, Spider Grandmother, left them and went out in the wilderness to live. She built a house for herself near the southern edge of the great Black Mesa, and there she stayed with her two boy grandchildren, Pokanghoya and Polongahoya. The boys were twins. They played together, and what one did the other also did. Sometimes they hunted rabbits for Spider Grandmother, but mostly they spent their days exploring the mesa country. They went first one way, then another, playing stick ball as they traveled. A time came when the boys became lonely for other people. They asked Spider Grandmother, "Are there no people in this country? Where can we find someone to talk to?"

Spider Grandmother said, "No, in this country there are only the three of us."

Still, the boys yearned to see other people. When they went on their wanderings, they would say to one another, "Let us go to the west—perhaps there is someone there," or, "Let us try the

top of the mesa—perhaps we shall find a village somewhere."
But wherever they went, there was nothing but endless land.
There were no people to be seen anywhere.

One day their wandering took them southward, and they
came to the spring that is called Lamehva. It was cool at the
spring, and because the earth around it was moist, many reeds
were growing at its edge. There, at the side of the spring,
Pokanghoya and Polongahoya began to play in the mud. They
made little mud houses. They made a little kiva. They made a
complete village of little houses, and after that they made little
mud people. They put their mud people here and there, in front
of the houses, in the kiva, and on the roofs. They had girls
grinding corn, women making piki, and men weaving cloth. The
people seemed real to the boys after a while, and they felt almost
as though they had discovered a living village.

When the sun was getting low in the sky they returned home.
Spider Grandmother scolded them, saying, "Where have you
been? It is late. You should have been here long ago."

"We went to the south," Pokanghoya said.

"We arrived at a spring," Polongahoya said.

"And did you find people there?" Spider Grandmother asked.

"No," they said, "there was no one there. But we made a village
out of mud."

Spider Grandmother said, "You see, it is just as I told you.
There are no people in this land."

When morning came the boys said, "We are going back to the
village we made."

But Spider Grandmother answered, "No, do not return there today. Let the sun harden the mud for a while."

Pokanghoya and Polongahoya said, "But we must see our people."

Spider Grandmother answered, "Wait a little. Let the mud dry. It is better that way. On the fourth day you may go back again."

So the boys went in another direction that day, wondering why Spider Grandmother wanted them to stay away so long from the spring. But on the morning of the fourth day they arose early. They said, "Now we are going back to see if our village has dried."

Spider Grandmother smiled at them. She said, "Yes, your village has dried."

The boys went to the south. They had almost arrived at the spring when Pokanghoya said, "I hear people talking."

Polongahoya said, "I also hear people talking."

Pokanghoya said, "It sounds as though they are at the spring."

Polongahoya said, "Let us climb higher to see."

They climbed some high rocks, and now they were able to see the place where they made their mud village. But the village they saw was not a small one made of mud. It was a large one, with real houses made of stone and with real people going this way and that. The houses, the kiva, everything looked just as they had made it, and everything was just where they had placed it. "See the girl grinding corn!" Pokanghoya said. "She is one that I made!"

"Yes," Polongahoya said, "and the man coming out of the kiva, I put him there!"

"Grandmother has done this," they said. "This is what she meant by drying."

They approached a little closer, and as they did so a man sitting on a rooftop called out, "Kiavakovi! Someone is coming."

The people looked up and saw the boys. The chief of the village said, "Welcome them. They are our first visitors."

And from every house someone called out, "Come in, come in! Sit down and rest yourselves!"

Pokanghoya and Polongahoya entered a house. The people gave them sweet corn and melons to eat. And when the boys were finished there, they went into another house, and there also the people gave them food. They entered every house in the village, and every family fed them. The chief took them into the kiva, and they talked together. And at last when the sun was descending in the west, the boys returned home, taking with them much piki bread that the people had given them.

Spider Grandmother said, "Did you find your village doing well?"

They said, "Grandmother, it was doing well."

She asked, "Was it dried?"

They said, "Grandmother, it was truly dried."

She asked, "And was there someone to talk to?"

They answered, "Yes, we talked to everyone. They gave us this piki to bring with us."

Spider Grandmother said, "Well, now you know how it is. I

brought your village to life so that you would no longer be lonely. The village will be called Lamehva, just as the spring is called Lamehva. And because of the reeds that grow there, the people shall belong to the Reed Clan. You are the ones who shaped them out of mud and loneliness. Therefore, you must always think of them as your children. They shall be dear to you. You must treat them well forever."

Pokanghoya and Polongahoya said, "Yes, this is the way it will be."

So it was that the village of Lamehva and the Reed Clan people were shaped by Pokanghoya and Polongahoya and brought to life by Spider Grandmother.

Not far from Lamehva, a little higher up on the mesa, were two tall rocks that the people called Kaiotakwi, Burnt Corn, because they resembled ears of darkened maize. The years went by, and in time some other people came and built a village at Kaiotakwi. Then there were two villages, one below and one above. Life was much the same in the two villages except for one thing. In Kaiotakwi they had a cat to help them with their hunting. For the people of Kaiotakwi the hunting was good because the cat helped them greatly. But the hunters of Lamehva had nothing to help them, and it was hard to get meat.

The chief of Lamehva had a son named Sikakokuh. The boy pondered on the hard times that the Lamehva hunters were having, and one night he went to the kiva to speak with his father.

He said, "My father."

The chief replied, "My son."

The boy said, "There is a thing to speak of."

His father said, "Let us speak of it."

"Up above, in the village of Kaiotakwi," the boy said, "they have a cat to help them catch rabbits and other game."

"Yes, it is so," his father said.

"We also should have something to help us hunt," Sikakokuh said.

"It would be good," his father answered.

"Where, then," the boy asked, "can we find something even better than a cat?"

The chief puffed on his pipe. He thought a long while. At last he said, "I have heard that in a place far to the east, called Suchaptakwi, there are dogs. They are larger than cats, and better hunters."

The boy said, "Good. Let us have a dog for our village."

His father answered, "It is not an easy thing. The distance is far, and there are many dangers. There are guards along the trail, and visitors to Suchaptakwi are turned away. Besides, who would make the journey?"

"I will go," the boy said. "I will get the dog, and he will help our village hunt."

"Very well," the chief said, "this is the way it will be. It is settled."

So the men of the village set to work making prayer sticks for Sikakokuh to carry with him. The boy's sisters began to prepare food for him to eat on the journey. Sikakokuh slept. Morning came, and he went out of the village and followed a trail to the east. In time he came to a place of tall pine trees, and there Spider Grandmother was waiting for him.

She said, "At last you are here. I have been expecting you, for it was I who breathed this journey into your mind. There are dangers on the way to Suchaptakwi. There is much to be understood. Therefore, I am going with you."

The boy said, "I am grateful."

Then Spider Grandmother made herself small, and in the form of a spider she climbed up and sat on Sikakokuh's ear, saying, "Whenever there is something that needs to be done, I will tell you."

The boy continued his journey to the east. He came to a place where a rattlesnake guarded the trail. The snake sounded his rattles. When he spoke, it was with an angry voice. He said, "Turn back. No one may pass this way."

Spider Grandmother whispered in the boy's ear, "Give him a prayer stick."

Sikakokuh selected a prayer stick and placed it on the ground before the rattlesnake. He said, "Accept this prayer stick made by the people of my village."

The rattlesnake's anger melted away. He accepted the prayer stick. He said, "For what you have given me I am glad. Therefore, you may go on. Follow the trail to Suchaptakwi."

So the boy passed by. And after a while he saw a large bear

standing in his path. The bear spoke fiercely. He said, "Turn back. No one may go beyond this point."

"Give him a prayer stick," Spider Grandmother whispered.

The boy presented a prayer stick to the bear, saying, "I bring you a new prayer stick made by my people."

The bear became gentle. He said, "For this prayer stick I am grateful. You may pass."

The boy went on, and after a while he met a large buck deer. The buck menaced Sikakokuh with his antlers. He said, "Go back. This is a forbidden trail."

Again Spider Grandmother told the boy to offer a prayer stick, and when the buck had received it he said, "Thank you. You may pass."

But Spider Grandmother whispered, "Wait. Do not go on yet. We must borrow his antlers."

Sikakokuh said, "Uncle, we have great need of your antlers."

The buck answered, "Yes, you may have them for a while. Twist them gently, and they will come off. Take them. When you return, leave them here in this tree where I can find them again."

The boy twisted the antlers and removed them. Then he resumed the journey.

In time he came to a high mountain. Its sides were slippery. Whenever the boy tried to go up, he slid back. Spider Grandmother said, "Use the antlers as walking sticks." And using the antlers this way, bracing the points against the slippery trail, Sikakokuh went slowly up the mountainside. When at last he was near the top he heard a strange barking sound.

He said to Spider Grandmother, "What is the sound I hear?"

She replied, "It is the voice of the thing for which you have made your journey. That is the sound of a dog."

He went on quickly then, and when he reached the crest of the mountain, he saw the dog. It ran back and forth, barking. It turned and trotted ahead of Sikakokuh, leading him to what appeared to be a water hole. Protruding out of the water was the top of a ladder. The dog began to descend the ladder, and as he did so the water disappeared.

"Follow him," Spider Grandmother said. "This is the kiva of the dog people."

Sikakokuh followed. He went down the ladder and found himself in a large kiva, just as Spider Grandmother had said. Above his head water again covered the entrance.

A man was sitting in the kiva smoking his pipe. He said, "Well, you have arrived at last. We have been expecting you. Our messengers told us you were coming. Sit down with me and smoke."

The boy sat down. He received the pipe from the man and smoked a while. Then he returned the pipe.

The man said, "You have traveled a long way. Why are you here?"

Sikakokuh answered, "Yes, it is true. I have traveled far. In my village we hunt rabbits and other game for meat, but the hunting is hard. We do not have enough to eat. In another village nearby the people have a creature they call a cat. It helps them when they go hunting. But we have heard that dogs are the best of hunters. We need a dog in our village. That is why I have come to Suchaptakwi."

The man considered what he had heard. He laid his pipe aside, saying, "Rest and refresh yourself now. I will think about it." He called for food for the boy. Girls came from another room in the kiva bringing corn, melon, and fruit. The boy ate. And after he was finished he sat waiting for the man to speak.

The man said, "I am the first uncle of the dogs. But there is another uncle who must be consulted. I have sent for him."

Spider Grandmother whispered, "The uncle who is coming, he is a hard man. He speaks roughly. You must persuade him."

The second uncle arrived. He said, "Why is this stranger in our kiva?"

The first uncle said, "He comes from the village of Lamehva. He wants a dog to take home with him."

The second uncle said, "It is here in Suchaptakwi that dogs are meant to live. They will remain here forever."

The boy spoke then. He said, "Uncle, the people of my village made these prayer sticks for you." He handed three prayer sticks to the man. Then he went on: "In Lamehva the people are suffering because they don't have enough meat. We go hunting for rabbits. Sometimes we find them in their burrows, so we have a little meat. When we see them running away, we use our throwing sticks, but it is difficult. Often we go home with hardly anything. In the upper village of Kaiotakwi the people are more fortunate because they have a cat that helps them hunt. My father, the chief of Lamehva, told me that the dog people live here. He told me that dogs are the best of hunters. If we have a dog in our village our life will be better. Therefore, I have come. It was a long journey."

The second uncle said, "You are courageous to have made this journey. And I am glad for the prayer sticks. Because of these things and because of what you have told me, you may take one dog with you to Lamehva." After saying this, he left the kiva.

The first uncle of the dogs said, "Now it is arranged. It will be done this way: We shall have a dance. You will see all the dogs, and you will select one to take home with you." He sent a message to an inner room of the kiva telling the dog people to prepare for the dance. The dancers made themselves ready. They went to where their dog pelts were hanging on the wall. As a man or a woman put on his pelt, he became transformed into a dog. All the people became dogs. They came to the center of the kiva, formed a line, and began to dance. As they danced they sang:

> "Wa waha-o waha, waha!
> Wa-a waha-o waha o-ha hala ena!"

They danced all night, until the rising of the sun. Sikakokuh watched them, wondering, "Shall I take this one? Or shall I take that one?" Some were large, some were small. Some had long fur, some had short. Some were black, some were brown, some were spotted. Sikakokuh could not decide. At last, when the dancing came to an end, the first uncle of the dogs said, "You have seen them all. Now make your choice."

Sikakokuh looked at the largest dog, but Spider Grandmother whispered, "Not that one, take the small one at the end." The boy looked at the small one. It was only a puppy. Spider Grandmother said again, "Take the small one."

So the boy said, "Yes, I have decided. I want the little one with the spots in back."

The man nodded his head, saying, "You must have great understanding of these things, for the one you have chosen is the fastest and best hunter among us. Very well, he is yours. Take him back with you to your village."

The boy took the puppy gently and held it. He fed it, and they became friends. The other dogs went back to the inner room and took off their dog pelts. They became people again. Everyone slept. When morning came, Sikakokuh prepared to leave.

The first uncle said to the boy, "You have chosen one of our people to go with you. He will grow into a good watchdog and a great hunter. Treat him well. Speak to him gently. Never strike him, never abuse him. If you treat him well, he will bring good luck to your village. Whoever abuses him will suffer in return. Anyone who strikes the dog will become crippled in his legs. If something should happen and the dog dies, you must bury him as you would bury one of your own people. But he will not remain in the ground where you bury him. After four days he will return to us here in Suchaptakwi to live again with us in our kiva."

"Uncle, I will remember," Sikakokuh said. Carrying the puppy in his arms, he ascended the ladder. As he neared the top, the cover of water dissolved, and when he had passed through the opening, the water reappeared. From the outside the entrance to the kiva again looked like an ordinary water hole.

The boy began his return journey. He came to the place where he had left the buck deer, and he hung the antlers in a tree. He went on, and again he met the bear and the rattlesnake who guarded the trail. And when he came to the place where he had met Spider Grandmother, she left him and he continued on with his dog. As he approached his village he saw his two sisters standing on a high rock waiting for him. Every day since his departure they had come there to watch for his return.

Sikakokuh put the puppy on the ground. He said, "Here is our dog."

The girls were glad, but they asked, "Can such a one as this truly hunt?"

They reached home. The girls called out, "Mother," and their mother came out of the house. They called, "Father," and their father came out. Other people came. They looked in wonder at the dog.

The chief said, "My son, I see you have brought something with you."

The boy answered, "My father, I have brought him. Now we have a dog to help us."

The people of the village crowded around. They touched the dog and rubbed his fur, saying, "So this is what a dog looks like." They spoke to him gently, as though he were a child. The next

day there was a ceremony. The dog's hair was washed, and they gave him a name, Tintopako-koshi, meaning Spotted-in-Back.

Time passed, and a day came when Spotted-in-Back was old enough to go hunting. The men and boys went out to look for meat, and they took Spotted-in-Back with them. What they saw greatly surprised them, for Spotted-in-Back could pick up the scent of a rabbit and follow him swiftly. He caught many rabbits and brought them back to the hunters. That day no hunter went home without meat. And afterwards when they went hunting again, things were the same. Good fortune had come to the village of Lamehva.

But in the upper village, Kaiotakwi, the people heard what had happened and they were jealous, for they had only a cat to help them. They became angry with the people of Lamehva. As for the dog, they said to one another, "He is an evil creature, he steals all the game."

Things went on this way. When he was not hunting, Spotted-in-Back went here and there exploring the countryside. He went up on the buttes, he followed the washes, and he wandered on the mesa. And one night when everyone was asleep, he found his way into the upper village and prowled among the houses. He found some meat hanging there, and he ate it. Day came again. People discovered that their meat had been stolen. The next night more meat disappeared, and the next night also. The people of Kaiotakwi examined the ground and found the tracks left by the dog. They were very angry. They said, "It was the evil creature from Lamehva. Let us put bait out for him tonight and wait for him. We will catch him and destroy him."

They prepared the bait. They put a piece of meat out in the courtyard of the village. And as the night came, the men hid on the rooftops with sticks and clubs in their hands. They waited. There was a bright moon, and late in the night they saw the dark shadow of the dog moving across the courtyard. Spotted-in-Back came to the meat and began eating. The men jumped down from their hiding places and surrounded him. They began to beat him. Spotted-in-Back could not escape. They killed him. Then they took his body to the edge of the village and threw it away.

Morning came. In Lamehva they looked for Spotted-in-Back. They could not find him. "He is on the mesa," someone said. "He will return soon." The sun rose higher, but still the dog did not come. "Perhaps he is hunting by himself down below," someone suggested. But Spotted-in-Back did not return. So they began looking for him, following his tracks. At last they found his body where the people of Kaiotakwi had left it. The people of Lamehva were grieved.

The boy Sikakokuh went to his father. He said, "A terrible thing has happened. We have lost Spotted-in-Back, our friend and helper. The people of Kaiotakwi have killed him. Once again our hunting will be difficult and our lives hard."

The chief replied, "It is an evil thing they have done. Who can live with people who do such things?"

They took the body of Spotted-in-Back to the foot of a great rock, and there they buried it as the dog people had instructed them to do. They put stones around the grave and left food and prayer sticks there just as though they had buried a person of their own family. Then they returned to their homes.

For the next four days the people of Lamehva did nothing. They did not work in their fields, they did not weave, they made no pottery, they ground no corn. They merely sat in their houses or their kiva mourning the death of their friend. At daybreak on the fourth day they returned to the place where they had buried Spotted-in-Back. He was not there. The grave was empty. They saw the marks of his feet on the ground, and the tracks led to the east. They followed his tracks for a while, then they returned.

Sikakokuh said, "It is just as the uncle of the dogs said it would be. Spotted-in-Back has gone back to be with his own people in Suchaptakwi."

Henceforth there were angry feelings between the villages of Lamehva and Kaiotakwi. If a person from Lamehva met a person from Kaiotakwi, neither would speak to the other. They merely passed in silence. And soon a strange thing happened in Kaiotakwi. The men who had killed the dog became lame. Their knee joints swelled, and they could go from one place to another only with the help of walking sticks. For this misfortune they blamed the village of Lamehva. "The people of Lamehva are sorcerers," they said.

In Lamehva the men gathered in the kiva and discussed the state of affairs. "We cannot live in this place any more," a man said. "It is like a sickness to be so close to Kaiotakwi." Another said, "Yes, that is the way it is. The name Kaiotakwi leaves a bitter taste in the mouth." Another said, "We must find another home. Let us follow the tracks of Spotted-in-Back. There, somewhere in the east, we will build another village." All night long they talked. And when morning dawned the people went to their houses and prepared for their journey.

Whatever they could carry with them they carried. What they could not carry they left behind. They started out together, following the tracks of the dog. The people of Kaiotakwi saw them leave. But then a heavy mist came down from the sky and covered the people of Lamehva so that they were no longer visible. In the heart of the mist they journeyed eastward, until at last they came to a place called Koechapteka on a broad shelf of land just below the heights of the great mesa. There they stopped. The mist that covered them lifted, and they saw that it was a good land. So they built a new village, and on the lower ground they planted their fields. They began to live in peace once more.

The years came, one after another, and in time strange tribes arrived from the north. Sometimes these tribes made war on the village. The Navahos came. The Paiutes and the Apaches came. So once more the people had to move. Above them, on the heights of the mesa, was the village of Walpi, which in ancient times had been settled by the Fire Clan. Walpi stood at the very rim of steep cliffs that protected it on all sides against attack by enemy warriors. The people of Koechapteka sent messengers to ask permission to come and live in Walpi. The elders of Walpi met in the kiva and considered the matter, and they agreed to receive the people from the settlement down below. Koechapteka was abandoned then, and the people took all the possessions they could carry and went up to the top of the mesa, where they were given a place to build their houses. Walpi remains there yet on the heights, and from the rim of the mesa people can still look down upon the ruins of Koechapteka.

This is the story of the Reed Clan, the people who were shaped by Pokanghoya and Polongahoya out of mud at the spring called Lamehva, and who were brought to life by Gogyeng Sowuti, Spider Grandmother. The spring where they were created still flows, and not far away are the ruins of the village of Kaiotakwi in the shadow of the Burnt Corn rocks. Some of the clans say they still have more migrations to make. But the Reed Clan people of Walpi say they will stay in Walpi forever.

The Beetle's
Hairpiece

❖

A beetle that lived near Oraibi often went to the outskirts of the village to find food. One day he was exploring there to find a grain of corn or a piece of melon when the children of the village caught him. At first they played with him, then they began to make insulting remarks about his appearance. "Look," one of them said, "he has nothing to cover him, not even a hair." Another child said, "Yes, he is bald. A bald-headed beetle." They made jokes about how naked the beetle was. And when at last he escaped and went home, he was ashamed that he had no hair.

He thought, "Why is it that I am smooth and shiny? Everyone has hair except me." So he went into the forest and searched until he found the corpse of a deer. He carefully removed hairs from the hide. Later he found a tree from which sticky gum was dripping. He took some of the gum and returned home.

In the morning when it was time to go again to the village, he plastered the gum on his head, and on top of that he stuck the hairs from the deer hide. "Now," he said, "I am no longer bald." He went to the edge of Oraibi and began his search for food. Again the children came and found him. "Here is our beetle," one of them said, "but he looks different today." Another said, "See, he has hair on his head." Another said, "He smells of tree gum." Another said, "Yes, he has tree gum on his head under his hair." And because the children were fond of chewing tree gum, they pulled out the hair, scraped off the tree gum, and began to chew it. They let the beetle go, saying, "Oh, he is just as bald as ever."

The beetle was embarrassed. He returned to his house. He pondered, "How is it that even young children have hair while I who am old have none?" Again he went out and gathered a supply of deer hairs. Then he searched until he found a cactus. He broke off a cactus thorn and used it to pierce the plant at a soft place. White sap began to run out. He collected some of it and went home. The next morning he rubbed the cactus sap on his head and attached the deer hairs to it. Because he was more experienced now, he arranged the hairs well. He looked at himself in a nearby pool, thinking how handsome he was. After that he went to the village to look for food.

But the sun was very warm, and the cactus sap began to dry out and crack. When the children came, one of them said, "Here is our beetle again. See, he has grown more hair." They looked more closely and saw the dry cactus sap cracking and falling off in pieces. They laughed, saying. "No, he has no hair after all. It is falling off. He is just as bald as before."

Once more the beetle returned home. He thought, "Why is it that of all the people of Oraibi, I alone have no hair?"

Now, the beetle had heard that the next day there was to be a kachina dance in the village. Everyone would be there. He wished to go also, but he was ashamed to appear with a bald head. So he traveled a long way to a certain pine grove, and he collected some of the pine tar that was stuck to the bark. He found the carcass of a coyote and took some hairs. After this he went back to his house. Because the dancing was to start early in the morning, he decided to put on his hair before going to sleep. He rubbed the pine tar on his head and attached the coyote hairs to it. Then he slept.

When he awoke he was ready to go to Oraibi at once. But his head felt very heavy. He could not raise it. He tried again, but he could not move his head because in the cool of the night the pine tar had stuck to the ground and hardened. He struggled, but he could not budge from where he was lying.

In the distance he heard the voices of the kachina dancers and the sound of their tortoise-shell rattles. All day long the singing went on, but the beetle had to lie where he was. He would hear a certain song and say, "Now they are doing the Corn Dance." He would hear another song and say, "Now they are doing the Bean Dance." He would hear another song and say, "Now they are doing the Mountain Sheep Dance." Then he would struggle to get up, saying, "Now I am doing the Beetle Dance." But he could not get up. He remained helpless where he lay.

At last, late in the afternoon, the sunlight fell on him. Its warmth softened the pine tar, and he was able to free himself. He scraped his head clean, went to the top of his house like a village crier, and called out: "Hear me! From this day on all beetles shall be bald!"

And ever since then, that is the way it has been.

Joshokiklay
and the Eagle

❖

In Oraibi, it is said, the young boy Joshokiklay lived with his parents and his sister. He had two eagles, which he kept on the roof of the house. He had taken them from their nest when they were young, washed them, fed them, and cared for them as though they were his brothers. He went out frequently to hunt rabbits for them to eat. Now the eagles were full grown. One day Joshokiklay went hunting to get fresh meat for them. His father and mother went out to their field to weed corn. His sister remained behind to make piki bread. One of the eagles broke loose from the place where it was tied and came down to where she was working. It knocked over her bowl and spilled the piki batter on the ground. The girl became angry. She struck the eagle with a stick, killing it. She regretted what she had done and feared what would happen when it became known that she had killed her brother's eagle. So she buried the eagle under a mound of ashes. And when she finished making the piki, she went out to the field where her parents were working. She said nothing about what had happened.

46

Joshokiklay returned from hunting, bringing a rabbit for his eagles to eat. He climbed the ladder to the top of the house. He found only one eagle there. He said, "Where is my other brother whom I left here when I went hunting?"

The eagle answered, "Your other eagle brother is dead. Your sister was making piki, and he went down below where your sister was working and spilled her batter. She struck him with a stick and killed him. She buried him in the ashes."

Joshokiklay went down and found the dead eagle. He took its body to a place below the mesa and buried it there. He returned to his house and spoke to the eagle on the roof, saying, "What shall I do now? My other brother is dead."

The eagle replied, "Let us leave this place where our brother was killed. Put on your best clothes. Then we shall go."

The boy went inside and put on his kilt. He tied bands of bells to his ankles, and put his sash around him. He took his bow. Then he went to the roof and unfastened the cord that held the eagle to its perch. He got on the eagle's back. The eagle spread its wings and flew away, soaring above the cliffs. Joshokiklay looked down and saw his village far below. The eagle circled above the field where the boy's family was working. He circled lower and lower.

The father heard the tinkle of the bells on Joshokiklay's ankles and looked up, saying, "Do I hear the sound of ankle bells in the sky?"

The mother said, "It is only an eagle soaring there."

Joshokiklay's sister said, "That is my brother riding on the eagle's back." Then they all saw Joshokiklay. While they watched, the eagle began to move higher into the sky. It grew small in the distance. Then at last it disappeared from their sight.

The eagle continued upward until it came to a hole in the sky that led into the other world called Tokpela. They passed through the hole and continued upward. Joshokiklay saw that it was a land of buttes and mesas. At last the eagle alighted on the pinnacle of a tall spire of rock. "This is my home," he said. "Here you will stay."

Joshokiklay got off the eagle's back. There was no room for him to move one way or another, for on all sides there was nothing but sheer cliff. The eagle departed. Joshokiklay lay on top of the rock spire in fear lest he fall. Hunger and thirst came upon him. The day faded and night came, then day again, but the eagle did not return. Joshokiklay thought, "Why did my brother bring me here and leave me? I cannot go down. Hunger and thirst will kill me." He thought of his father and mother, fearing that he had seen them for the last time. And just when he thought that there was nothing left to hope for, a small wren alighted next to him on the rock.

The wren said, "Why are you here?"

Joshokiklay replied, "I was brought here by my eagle brother. He went away. I am hungry and thirsty."

The wren flew away, returning soon with a grain of corn in its mouth. "Eat this," the wren said, and it flew away again. Joshokiklay chewed on the grain of corn. When the wren returned once more, it had a drop of water in its mouth. It let the water trickle onto Joshokiklay's tongue. His hunger and thirst disappeared.

"Wait here," the wren said. "I am going to bring you down from this pinnacle." It flew down to the base of the towering rock. There it removed a feather from its back and stuck it into a crack. It removed another feather and placed it in a crack higher up. Stepping on these feathers as though they were rungs of a ladder, the wren mounted the high rock, placing more feathers as it climbed. At last it reached the summit, and by this time it was completely naked.

It said, "Now we shall go down."

Joshokiklay said, "How is it possible? We shall fall and be killed."

The wren said, "Trust me. Get on my back."

The boy mounted the wren's back, but he asked, "How shall we go down?"

"By the feather steps." And the wren began to descend, stepping from one feather to another. After they reached the ground, the wren went up again to reclaim all its feathers and place them back in its body. When it returned, it was fully clothed.

"Now," it said, "go that way, toward the west. There you will find someone to help you."

Joshokiklay walked for a long time, but he saw no village. He was tired, and he stopped to rest. As he began to sit down, he heard a voice say, "Do not sit on me." He looked around but saw no one. Again he started to sit down, and again the voice said, "Do not sit on me." This time he looked closely at the ground, and he saw her then. It was Gogyeng Sowuti, Spider Grandmother.

"I am sorry," Joshokiklay said. "I didn't see you."

"Sit over there," Spider Grandmother said, "and when you are rested, come into the house."

He rested, looking at the tiny hole in the ground that was the entrance to Spider Grandmother's house. He asked, "How shall I ever enter such a small doorway?"

Spider Grandmother said, "Sit here over the opening and wriggle like this."

He sat over the opening and wriggled, burrowing his way into the earth. He passed through the entrance and found himself inside. It was a kiva. Spider Grandmother fed him and cared for him, and Joshokiklay remained with her for many days.

Each morning Joshokiklay went hunting for antelope or deer, and he kept the kiva well supplied with food. They ate well, and Spider Grandmother was pleased with him. One evening as they sat together talking, Spider Grandmother said, "You are a good hunter. I do not know where you go in search of game, but I have to warn you about one thing. Do not go hunting to the north, for in that direction Hasokata the Gambler has his kiva. If a stranger passes that way, Hasokata forces him to gamble. Hasokata always wins, and those who play against him always die. Therefore, stay away from the north and do your hunting elsewhere."

Up to that time, Joshokiklay did not care where he went to hunt. But now he was curious about Hasokata the Gambler. Daylight came, and the boy took his bow and went hunting to the north. In time he discovered the entrance of Hasokata's kiva. He looked down. He saw Hasokata down below in the half-darkness. Hasokata saw Joshokiklay. He welcomed him. He said, "Come down. Enter the kiva and sit with me."

Joshokiklay went down the ladder. He sat with Hasokata. Hasokata lighted a pipe and puffed on it. He handed it to the boy. Joshokiklay puffed and returned the pipe. After a while Hasokata said, "Let us play a game."

Joshokiklay answered, "What game shall we play?"

Hasokata said, "Let us play the stick game."

Joshokiklay said, "Yes, I will play with you."

Hasokata brought out his totolospi sticks, made of split reeds. He said, "If you win, I will give up my life to you. If I win, you will give up your life to me. Is it understood?"

"It is understood," Joshokiklay said. "Let us begin."

Hasokata threw the sticks, then the boy threw the sticks, taking turns back and forth. Hasokata won the game. He said, "You have lost. Now you must pay." He removed the boy's clothes, tied him, and placed him on a ledge. He opened a small door in the wall of the kiva, and through it the north wind began to blow. The cold air rushed at Joshokiklay and chilled him. He said, "The cold enters my body. I am freezing."

While all this was happening, Spider Grandmother began to worry about Joshokiklay, and she went out to look for him. She went this way and that and finally came to the kiva of Hasokata the Gambler. Looking down through the kiva opening, she saw the boy lying on the ledge dying of the cold. She quickly found a small downy turkey feather, brought it into the kiva, and placed it on top of Joshokiklay to keep him warm. Because she was so small, Hasokata noticed nothing. Then Spider Grandmother returned to her own kiva. Now, Spider Grandmother belonged to the Kachina Clan. She stood on a high place and called for the people of her clan to assemble. Her voice carried into the distance, and the Kachinas heard. They came from every direction, each Kachina dressed the way he was supposed to be, wearing his kilt and his tortoise-shell rattle, his face painted, and his long hair falling over his shoulders. They descended into Spider Grandmother's kiva, and she told them about Hasokata and Joshokiklay. They discussed the matter. Then they went to Hasokata's place, entering the kiva by the ladder. The Kachinas asked Hasokata to let the boy go free.

"We played the stick game," Hasokata said, "and the boy lost. Therefore, he is mine."

The Kachinas said, "Let us have another contest. If you win, the boy belongs to you. If we win, he belongs to us."

Because he loved to gamble, Hasokata agreed, and the Kachinas then explained the game they would play. "You are master of the freezing wind," they said. "We can make things grow. The contest is this: We shall grow corn and squash and melons here on the floor of your kiva. Send your freezing wind to fight with them."

The contest began. The Kachinas sprinkled sand on the floor, and in the sand they planted seeds. They began to dance and sing to make the seeds sprout. Hasokata summoned the north wind to come and kill the sprouts. The air grew colder. Corn shoots sprouted. Squash shoots sprouted. Melon shoots sprouted. The north wind roared, but the corn stalks formed, the vines grew, and squash and melons formed on the vines. The north wind blew harder and harder, but it could not stop the growing. The Kachinas sang a song calling for thunder, lightning, and rain. Lightning came, thunder came, and the rain began to fall. The ground outside became heavy with water, which began to run down into the kiva. When the water reached the corn, melons, and squash, they grew even more rapidly than before. Hasokata was helpless against the powers of the Kachinas. He cried out, "Let us stop! You have won and I have lost!"

So the Kachinas untied Joshokiklay, gave him his clothes, and took him up the ladder. But the water continued to run into the kiva, which began to fill up. Only Hasokata remained there. He was singing a song to try to make the water stop coming. Each line of his song ended with a gulp as the water entered his mouth:

"Bye na mo geh kwing eu . . . *euc-a-euc!*
Bye na mo geh kwing eu . . . *euc-a-euc!*"

The Kachinas returned to their own homes, and Spider Grandmother took Joshokiklay back to her kiva. She told him that it was time to return to the other world from which he had come. She gave him a bundle of dried meat and led him to the opening that led from Tokpela to the world below. Joshokiklay looked through the opening. The distance was so far that he

could see nothing of his own land. He said, "How shall I ever descend?"

Spider Grandmother spun a web across part of the opening, and to it she attached a thread from her own body. The boy clung to her, and she let herself down by the thread the way spiders do. Descending like this, they finally reached the surface of Joshokiklay's world. Spider Grandmother returned to Tokpela, and Joshokiklay walked toward his village.

People in the fields saw him coming. They ran to his parents' house, saying, "Your son who was taken away by the eagle, he is returning."

His parents replied, "No, it cannot be Joshokiklay, for he was carried out of this world."

Others said, "Yes, it is true that Joshokiklay is coming back. See, he is coming through the fields."

His parents came out of their house. They saw him coming. They recognized him. They welcomed him as though he were returning from the land of the dead.

This is the story of Joshokiklay, who once had two eagles on the roof of his house and who was carried away to Tokpela through an opening in the sky.

Mockingbird Gives
Out the Calls

❖

In the beginning of things the birds were brought to life, but only Yaalpa, the mockingbird, had the knowledge of speech. It was the mockingbird who gave languages to the people when they emerged from the Lower World, and now he decided that the creatures of the air should also have a way of speaking. So one day he called them all together for a meeting.

He said, "All the tribes of men have their languages. When a Hopi speaks, it is with a Hopi voice. When an Apache speaks, you know him by the sound of his words. When a Navaho speaks, you know him to be a Navaho. The birds also should have languages. Since I am the one who has the knowledge of languages, I will give you the calls by which you will be recognized."

He addressed the rock hen, saying, "You, rock hen, your call shall be '*Chew! Chew! Chew!*' Wherever you are, whenever you wish to announce your presence, you will say, '*Chew! Chew! Chew!*' And whenever I want you to attend a meeting, I will call you by that sound."

The rock hen tried out his call, "*Chew! Chew! Chew!*" Then he flew off quickly, saying, "That's all I have to know."

Mockingbird spoke then to the red-tailed hawk. "You, red-tailed hawk, you will call out shrilly like this: '*Sieuuuu! Sieuuuu! Sieuuuu!*'"

"I hear what you say," the red-tailed hawk said. He tried out his call, "*Sieuuuu! Sieuuuu! Sieuuuu!*" And then he departed.

The mockingbird addressed the dove. "You, dove, you shall make a soft call like this: '*Hu-hu-huuu! Hu-hu-huuu!*'"

"*Hu-hu-huuu! Hu-hu-huuu!*" the dove said, and he flew away.

"You, owl," the mockingbird said, "you are to make a sound in your throat like this: '*G-hew! G-hew! G-hew!*'"

"Yes, I have it," the owl said. He, also, went away.

The mockingbird continued giving out calls, and as each bird learned what he was to say, he went home. Finally only the catbird remained. The mockingbird looked at him. He was surprised, for the two of them looked very much alike. "We appear to be cousins," the mockingbird said. "What kind of bird are you?"

"Yes," the catbird answered, "I am easily mistaken for you. I am the catbird."

"Well," the mockingbird said, "I will give you your call."

"No," the catbird said, "I don't think I want any call."

"Every bird should have its call," the mockingbird said.

"In this case it is different," the catbird answered. "From what I have seen, you are not very popular with the other birds. You are talking all the time. Too much talking drives people away. Did you notice how the birds left the meeting as soon as they could? They avoid you. You talk too much. I would rather not have a language. If I talk, the other birds may think I am you."

"But if I want to hold a meeting," the mockingbird said, "you will have to know your special call."

"No, it won't be necessary," the catbird replied. "If I hear you calling out 'G-hew!' for the owl and 'Sieuuuu!' for the red-tailed hawk, and all those other cries, then I will know there is to be a meeting and I will come."

"But," the mockingbird said, "how will you announce your presence when you arrive?"

"I'll just flutter my wings," the catbird said, and he flew away.

This is why the catbird says practically nothing. The only sound he makes is a faint "Miem!" He was ashamed of his cousin, the mockingbird, who talked too much, and when the calls were given out, he refused to accept one for himself.

The Boy Who
Crossed the Great Water
and Returned

❖

South and west of Oraibi there was once a village called
Sowituika. There were many boys in this village but not many
girls. The chief had one son, whose name was Dayveh. The chief
worried that his son would not find a wife. He often thought
about the matter. At last, one night, he asked his son to sit and
talk with him.

He said, "My son, there is something that must be done."

Dayveh answered, "My father, I am listening."

The chief said, "It is a difficult thing."

The boy replied, "Yes, I am ready. Tell me."

His father smoked silently for a while. Then he said, "I can
reveal it only a little at a time. But the first thing is this: You must
build your sinews and become a strong runner. Tomorrow you
will begin. Go to the edge of the village. Mark a spot. From
there, run toward the rising sun until you are too tired to go on.
Then return, running a little, walking a little, until you are
home."

In the morning the boy went to the edge of the village,

59

marked a place to begin, and ran toward the east. When at last he could run no more, he came back, walking a little, running a little, until he arrived at his starting place.

He said to his father, "I reached the place of the piñon trees, then I returned."

His father said, "That is good. Rest tomorrow, and on the second day run again."

That was the way it was thereafter, one day of running, one day of resting. Each time the boy went out he was able to run a little further than the time before. It went on like this for many days until Dayveh was able to reach a distant high rock and to return without stopping.

The chief said, "It is good. Your body grows stronger. Rest tomorrow, and after the sun has set I will tell you what comes next."

The next night Dayveh came and sat with his father. The chief smoked his pipe silently for a while. Then he went into another room and returned with a buckskin ball and a playing stick.

He said, "This is the second thing. You must become a good nahoydadatsya player. Tomorrow go out to the edge of the village and begin. Hit the ball as far as you can, follow it swiftly, hit it again, on and on this way until you are too tired to continue."

The next day the boy began. He struck the ball and raced after it, struck it again and followed it. Every second day he did this, resting on the days between. A time came when he moved almost as fast as the ball itself, and he was able at last to go to the same distant rock as before and to return without stopping.

The chief said, "It is good. Rest tomorrow, and when night comes I will tell you what is next."

So the next night Dayveh and his father again sat together. The chief smoked. After a while he went into another room and returned with his hunting bow and four arrows.

He said, "This is my bow. It is thick. It is meant for a man with strong arms. Take it. Practice with it. In the late afternoon when the sun is sliding down, go to the west of the village. Face the setting sun and shoot an arrow as though at the sun itself. When the arrow disappears into the redness of the sun, perhaps you will not see it any more. But in your mind you must follow its flight. In your mind, observe where it lands. Do this with the second arrow, the third, and the fourth. Consider where the arrows have come to rest, then follow them and find them. Shoot again into the face of the sun. Bend the bow as far as you can. Follow the arrows. Find them."

Dayveh said, "I will do it."

He slept, he awoke. And as the sun began to go down in the west he went out with the bow and the four arrows and began. He did not have the strong arms of his father, and the bow was hard to bend. The first arrows he shot did not go far. But as the days passed, his arms grew stronger, and his arrows went further and further. Each time he shot into the glare of the sun he followed the arrow in his mind. And a time came when he knew exactly where each arrow would be, even though his eyes could not see it in flight.

The chief said, "It is good. Now you are ready."

Dayveh said, "Ready for what, Father?"

The chief replied, "Tomorrow we shall sit and talk. Then I will tell you."

The night passed and day came. In the evening the chief sat smoking his pipe. Dayveh came and sat beside him.

The chief said, "My son."

The boy said, "My father."

The chief said, "This is the night to tell you what lies ahead. These things at which you have trained, there is a purpose in them. You are going on a long journey."

Dayveh replied, "I hear you. But I did not know that I was to go on a journey. Where am I going?"

His father said, "Yes, now is the time to reveal it." And he began: "Early tomorrow you will travel toward the west. You will come to the place where the trail ends. But you must continue on, running swiftly toward where the sun sets. It is for this journey that you have made yourself strong. In time you will see a large blue hill in the distance. Go there. As the blue color of the hill turns green, you will know that you are coming close. At last you will reach the hill. Go up and stand at the top. From there you will see where the land ends and the great water begins. Go forward to the edge of the water. Brace your heels in the sand. You will have two arrows with you. In your mind try to picture the land that lies beyond. Bend your bow hard, and shoot your first arrow across the great water. Follow its flight in your mind, and fix in your memory the place where it comes to earth in the land beyond."

The chief smoked his pipe silently, then he continued: "A strange thing will happen. The water will part in front of you. There will be a path. Enter it. Run as swiftly as you can. Before you the water will open; behind you it will close again. If you are not swift enough the water will swallow you. In time you will reach the other side. There you will find your arrow. Leave it there to mark the place of your return journey."

The chief stopped. He said nothing more.

Dayveh waited, and at last he said, "My father, why am I going on this journey?"

The chief answered, "My son, there is no wife for you in our village. There are many boys but only a few girls. Perhaps on this journey you will find a wife for yourself. Perhaps you will find wives for others. I cannot tell you any more."

Dayveh spoke again, saying, "When I have reached the other side of the great water, what must I do next?"

His father answered, "I cannot tell you. When you have arrived, it will be you who must decide."

Dayveh said, "I did not know it would be like this. I did not know I would have to go away."

He went to his sleeping place, but for a long while he could not sleep. He could only think of the strange journey. When at last he slept, his dreams were troubled. Dayveh's father did not sleep. He made prayer sticks and prayed throughout the night.

Dayveh's mother did not sleep. She made piki bread and ground sweet corn for Dayveh to carry with him.

In the morning the chief awakened his son. He dressed him in special clothes. He gave him new moccasins. He put a white kachina kilt around Dayveh's waist. He gave him a blue shirt of ancient style and put a woven belt around him. He tied small leg belts below Dayveh's knees and hung turquoise beads around his neck. Dayveh's mother combed his hair in the ancient style, and his father placed a white feather in it. On his shoulder they hung a water jug, a knapsack, and a quiver holding two arrows. His father handed him the hunting bow, saying, "It is time. Let us begin." He walked with Dayveh to the edge of the village.

"Here it starts," the chief said. "You must be back by the evening of the fourth day. I will come here and wait. If I do not see you by the time the sun has set, I will know that you are not returning. Go now, and run as you have trained yourself to run."

Dayveh followed the trail to the west. A time came when the trail disappeared, but Dayveh continued on. The sun rose high in the sky. The blue hill appeared in the distance. The sun moved, but still the hill remained blue. When Dayveh became hungry he took food from his knapsack and ate as he ran. At last, slowly, the blue hill began to turn green, and he knew that he was approaching it. He came to the hill and went up. For the first time since leaving the village he stopped running. He stood there at the top and saw the shore of the great water. He looked for land on the other side, but there was nothing but water to be seen.

He rested a while. Then he went down to the water's edge. He took an arrow from his quiver and placed it in the bow. He dug his heels in the sand to brace himself. He drew the cord back, and in his mind he pictured the land beyond. He released the arrow and watched it mount into the sky, arching like a rainbow, until at last it disappeared into the glare of the setting sun. In his mind he saw it fall on the shore beyond the sea.

The great water parted in front of him, revealing a path. Without hesitating, Dayveh entered, running swiftly. On each side of him the water rose in a great wall. Ahead of him the water continued to open, and behind him it closed with a roar. The distance was long. His legs became tired and his breath became thick, but he ran on and on without faltering. And just when he felt he could run no more, he came to land. The roar behind him died. He turned. There was no longer a path, only water as far as he could see. Dayveh rested on the beach. Afterwards, he found his arrow half buried in the sand. He left it there to mark the place where he had crossed. Then he went on till he reached the crest of a hill from where he could see in all directions. The land around him seemed wild and uninhabited. He was too tired to go further. He found a cave, and there he slept.

The red sun rose. Dayveh ate a little piki and drank from his water jug. Again he went to the top of the hill to look for signs of a village. Before him was a desert, but in the distance he could see the form of a mesa. He thought, "If people live in this land, it is there they will have their village." And so he went on in that direction. When the sun was directly above him he had not yet arrived. But in the afternoon, at last, he came to the foot of the mesa. He saw a man coming down to meet him.

The man approached Dayveh. He said, "You are a stranger?"

Dayveh answered, "I am a stranger in this country."

The man said, "Come up to the top of the mesa slowly. I will go ahead and announce to our chief that you are coming."

The man went on ahead, and when Dayveh reached the top of the trail, the man was waiting for him. They went to the chief's house. The chief welcomed Dayveh, and his wife brought food. The boy thought, "These are good people."

The sun was going down. The chief said to Dayveh, "Go out to the plaza now. The young people are playing games there."

Dayveh went out. The young people were playing nahoydadatsya, the girls on one side and the boys on the other. When they saw Dayveh they stopped, and a girl came to him and invited him to join in the game. They gave him a stick, and he played on the boys' side. But though Dayveh was the best player among the boys, the girls won. A girl came to him and said, "Because you have lost, you must give me your moccasins."

He gave them, and again they played and again the girls won the game. Another girl came to him and said, "You have lost. Therefore, you must give me your belt."

They played again, and again the girls won. Another girl came and took his turquoise beads. The games went on until Dayveh had lost everything he was wearing, including the feather from his hair. He returned to the chief's house, and the chief laughed when Dayveh entered. "Yes," he said, "it is evident. You have played and lost. This is the way it is in our village."

Dayveh slept. In the morning, he remembered that he had no clothes to put on. He was almost naked. His heart was lonely. When the chief and his wife sat down to eat their breakfast, they called on Dayveh to join them. He ate silently. While they were still eating there, a messenger came to the chief's house to announce that there would be a contest and that the champion runner of the village wished to race against Dayveh. The chief asked if Dayveh would accept the challenge. Dayveh accepted it. The chief said to the messenger, "It is arranged. Have the village crier call for the people to meet at the racing grounds."

The village crier went up to the highest roof and called out that the running contest was about to take place. The chief took Dayveh to the racing grounds and gave him a place to stand. He himself stood at another place with the village runner. As people arrived, the chief announced: "Those who are on our side, stand here with me. Those who choose to be on the stranger's side, stand over there with him." Everyone who heard the announcement went to stand with the chief. Dayveh stood alone. More people came. Nearly the entire village had arrived, and still Dayveh was alone. And then a small thin girl came. She heard the chief's announcement and saw Dayveh standing alone. She said, "I will go to the side of the stranger." She crossed over to where Dayveh was and stood beside him. Another girl, older than the small one, said, "I, too, will stand with the stranger." So in all the village there were only two people to stand with Dayveh and encourage him.

The chief went to the middle, halfway between the two sides. He stuck a knife in the ground and drew a circle around it with his finger. He said: "There are two runners. They will run to the distant knoll in the east, the one wearing a lone pine tree on its crest like a feather. The stranger will go around it to the right. My runner will go around it to the left. Then they will return." He spoke directly to Dayveh, saying, "You, if you win the race you may kill all of us who stand on this side. If my runner wins, I shall have the right to kill all of you who stand over there."

Dayveh said to the two girls, "I did not know it would be this way."

The girls said to him, "The village runner has powerful medicine. If you see him draw a circle on the ground, avoid that spot. Do not run across it."

The race toward the distant knoll in the east began. The village runner was larger than Dayveh, and his legs were built strongly. From the very start the village runner was ahead and Dayveh behind. Dayveh thought, "My father could not have foreseen my troubles. They are too great." Though the village runner was far ahead, Dayveh ran hard. He thought, "This may be my last race, but I will run as never before." He remembered the two girls who came to his side. Thinking of them gave him courage. He saw the village runner, far ahead of him, stop for a moment to mark a circle on the ground with his finger. Knowing it to be sorcery, when Dayveh came to the place he went around it. Again the village runner marked a spot, and again Dayveh moved aside and passed it by. Though his lungs pained him and his legs ached, he did not stop running. They came at last to the knoll in the east. The village runner went to the left and disappeared. Dayveh ran to the right. They passed each other on the far side. When Dayveh had circled the knoll he looked for the other runner, but he did not see him. Running ahead of him now was not a boy but a deer.

Dayveh said to himself, "Now I see how it is. Who can outrun a deer?" But he kept on, and after a while he noticed that the deer was tiring. The distance between them grew smaller. The deer looked back and saw Dayveh approaching. He ran around in a circle and then continued his way toward the village. Dayveh went to one side and avoided the circle. The deer was breathing heavily. Dayveh passed him, saying, "Now I shall run first and you can follow." But the deer tried hard and again took the lead, and again he went around in a circle to work sorcery against Dayveh. Dayveh avoided the place, and once more he saw the deer falter. He passed him. He went on. The deer was hardly moving now. The space between them grew longer and longer. Dayveh saw the villagers ahead. He came to the place where the race had started. It was over.

The chief was silent. All his people were silent. At last the village runner arrived. He was no longer a deer but a boy again, and he was walking slowly. Dayveh went to stand with his two friends. A girl approached him from the other side, holding out the moccasins she had taken from him the evening before.

Another girl brought his woven belt. Another brought his kilt. One by one all the things they had taken from him were returned, including the feather from his hair. He accepted his clothes and put them back on. But the people remained silent, looking now at the knife that the chief had stuck in the ground.

Dayveh picked up the knife. He said to the chief: "It is you who are responsible. I am a stranger here. I came in peace. Though I offended no one, the village mistreated me. You tried to win the race by sorcery as an excuse to kill me. It was you who placed the knife here and said, 'Whoever loses, he and all those who stand with him will die.' If my father, the chief of Sowituika, were here, I would ask him what I should do. But he is not here. I am alone from my village, and I must decide alone what to do."

He called the chief to come forward, and he killed him. He said to the others, "You people, I do not want to kill any more of you. Instead, I will take some of your girls and young women back to my village. There they will find husbands." The people agreed, and Dayveh went among them, selecting this girl and that, saying, "Go, stand over there with my two friends." He finished with the choosing. He said, "All you other people, go into your houses and remain there until we have gone." The people returned to the village and entered their houses. To the girls he had chosen, Dayveh said, "Go and prepare food for the journey." And when the food had been prepared, Dayveh took the hands of the two girls who had befriended him, saying, "Now let us go."

Dayveh's two friends said, "Let us not stop running, even when we become tired, because the men of the village will soon come after us." And what they told Dayveh was true, because in the village the men were forming a war party. They took their weapons and began to pursue.

When Dayveh and the girls reached the shore of the great water they stopped to rest, and Dayveh explained what was to come next. "When the water opens," he said, "we must run without stopping until we reach the other side." He found the arrow that marked the place where he had come ashore. He took his second arrow from his quiver. He braced his feet in the sand and drew the bow. The arrow shot into the sky, became small in the distance, and disappeared. Suddenly the water opened in front of them. "Run now!" Dayveh commanded. "There is no time to dream!"

They ran between the towering walls of water. There were many girls, and some of them were not as fast as others. Dayveh ran back and forth, first helping one girl, then another. If a girl began to tire he took her by the hand and pulled her along. Those who thought of stopping looked over their shoulders and saw the water reaching out for them, and they ran with new strength. In time they reached the other side. When they looked back toward the place from which they had come, the path had disappeared. They rested. They ate a little piki and quenched their thirst with water from their jugs. But Dayveh's two friends, the girls who had sided with him at the race, said, "We do not have time to rest any longer. At this moment the men of the village are pursuing us." So they went on.

On the other side of the water, the war party followed the footprints of Dayveh and the girls down to the shore.

One man said, "How can we follow? Ahead of us is nothing but water."

Another said, "It is hopeless. Let us go back."

But an old man said, "The ancient ones spoke of a tunnel beneath the sea."

Someone replied, "No, that is only old people's talk."

The old man said, "What the ancient ones told us is true. The entrance to the tunnel is covered with a giant clam shell. Let us search for it."

So the men searched along the shore, and at last one of them cried out, "Here is a giant clam shell! Who has ever seen a shell so large?" They gathered around it. Together they lifted it, and underneath they found the tunnel entrance. They went in, the younger men first and the older men following. In time they came to the other end. It, too, was covered by a giant clam shell. They pushed it aside and came out. They looked back at the water, saying, "Who would have imagined it? We were on the other side, and now we are in a strange land." They hunted until they found the tracks of Dayveh and the girls, and went on with the pursuit. The men in the war party were stronger than the girls, and slowly they gained ground on them. The warriors stopped when darkness came, because they could no longer see the footprints, but when the sun rose they followed again.

It was now the fourth day, and in the village of Sowituika the chief was concerned about the return of his son. Many times he went out and looked across the land, but he saw nothing. So he went to the top of his house and called for his messenger who lived in the east. The messenger came. It was a dove. The chief said, "I fear for my boy. He should now be returning. Fly toward the place where the sun goes down and tell me what you find."

The dove went flying to the west. In time he saw Dayveh and the girls running. He went on. He saw the war party in pursuit. He returned to the chief's house. He said, "I have found your son. He has many girls with him, but they are tired and cannot go rapidly any more. First your son helps one of them, then another. I flew on. I discovered a war party in pursuit. The men are running with strong legs."

The chief pondered. He went to the top of his house and called for his messenger who lived in the north. The messenger came. It was an owl. The chief instructed the owl this way: "In the direction of the setting sun my boy is returning from across the great water. With him he has girls who will find husbands in our village. Behind them is a war party. Take this medicine pipe which I have prepared. Go out and find my son. But do not stop there. Go on until you see the men who are following him. Smoke this pipe, and blow the smoke down in front of them."

The owl took the pipe and flew toward the west. He saw Dayveh and the girls. He went on until he saw the war party coming. Alighting on a high rock, he began smoking. The smoke came out of his mouth in a small black cloud. The cloud settled down and touched the earth. Then it exploded, spreading smoke in all directions. Every time the owl puffed, he sent out a small black cloud that descended to the earth, exploded, and spread a smoky darkness everywhere. It was as though a great fog had fallen on the earth. The men in the war party could not see the trail. They wandered around this way and that, and at last they huddled together in the darkness waiting for the strange fog to pass. The owl finished the pipe. He returned to the chief's house. He said, "I have done what you instructed me to do. The men are helpless for the moment, but they are close behind your son, and soon the smoke will blow away."

Again the chief went to the top of his house, and he called his messenger who lived in the south. While he waited, he piled wood on his fireplace. The fire burned hotly and covered the walls with soot. The messenger from the south arrived. It was a crow. He found the chief brushing hot soot from the walls. The chief gathered the hot soot into a pile. He said, "The war party that is pursuing my son is close. Take this soot and sprinkle it on them."

The crow placed the soot between his feathers. He flew away. He found the war party close behind Dayveh and the girls. He fluttered his feathers, and the hot soot sifted out and fell like black snow. The sunlight was blotted out. Down below, the men halted. The soot was falling all over them. It blistered their skin. They rubbed their arms and legs but could not brush the soot away. It fell in their hair and singed it, causing it to become short. Soot was everywhere. When he had done his work the crow returned home. Slowly the air became light again. The men looked at one another. One said, "Your skin is black." Another said, "Yours also is black." Another said, "The blackness will not come off." Another said, "What has happened? We once had long hair but now it is short." They discussed the strange thing that had occurred. And even as they talked to one another, their language changed. They no longer spoke Hopi, but another tongue instead.

Ahead of them they could see Dayveh and the girls. Greatly angered by their new misfortune, the men hurried to catch up with them. Dayveh saw them coming. He knew that because the girls were tired they would soon be captured. So he said to them, "The men are coming rapidly. There is no escape from them. So here we shall leave one another. I will take two of you with me. All the rest will wait for the men, and they will take you home."

Dayveh took the hands of his two friends, the girls who had come to help him on the other side of the water, and the three of them went on toward the east. The others waited. The men of their village came. The girls were afraid because they didn't recognize them any more. The men and the girls, except the two that Dayveh had with him, returned to the tunnel that led back to their own country.

Dayveh arrived at the place where his father was waiting. He said, "My father."

The chief said, "My son."

Dayveh said, "What you instructed me to do, I have done it. I crossed to the other side of the great water. I found a village. The people there treated me badly. But these two girls were my friends when the chief wanted to kill me. Because I won the race,

it was he, not I, who died. I brought many girls with me to be brides in our village. But they were too tired to go on. Therefore, I left them behind. But these two, I would not leave them. They are dear to me. The elder one, I will take her for my wife. The younger one, she will be my sister."

The chief was glad. He said, "It is good."

This is the story of how Dayveh, the chief's son, went across the great water and returned.

The old people say that the men of the war party, their skins blackened forever, became the ancestors of another race of men who today live beyond the sea.

Coyote and the
Crying Song

❖

Coyote once lived on Second Mesa near the village of Shipaulovi. The dove also lived near Shipaulovi. It was harvest time, and the dove was in the field collecting the seeds of the kwakwi grass. To separate the seeds from the stalks, she had to rub the tassels vigorously. But the kwakwi grass was sharp, and the dove cut her hands. She began to moan: "Hu-hu-huuu! Hu-hu-huuu! Ho-uuu, ho-uuu, ho-uuu!"

It happened that Coyote was out hunting, and he heard the voice of the dove. To Coyote, the moaning sounded like music. "What a fine voice," he said to himself, approaching the place where the dove was working. He stopped nearby, listening with admiration as the dove moaned again: "Hu-hu-huuu! Hu-hu-huuu! Ho-uuu, ho-uuu, ho-uuu!"

Coyote spoke, saying, "The song is beautiful. Sing it again."

The dove said, "I am not singing, I am crying."

Coyote said, "I know a song when I hear one. Sing it once more."

"I am not singing," the dove said. "I was gathering seeds from the kwakwi grass and I cut myself. Therefore, I am crying."

78

Coyote became angry. "I was hunting," he said, "and I heard your song. I came here thinking, 'The music is beautiful.' I stood and listened. And now you tell me you are not singing. You do not respect my intelligence. Sing! It is only your voice that keeps me from eating you. Sing again!"

And now, because she feared for her life, the dove began once more to moan: "Hu-hu-huuu! Hu-hu-huuu! Ho-uuu, ho-uuu, ho-uuu!"

Coyote listened carefully. He memorized the song. And when he thought he had it in mind, he said, "First I will take the song home and leave it there safely. Then I will continue hunting."

He turned and ran, saying the words over and over so that he would not forget them. He came to a place where he had to leap from one rock to another, but he missed his footing and fell. He got to his feet. He was annoyed. He said, "Now I have lost the song." He tried to remember it, but all he could think of was "Hu-hu."

So he went back and said angrily to the dove, "I was taking the song home, but I fell and lost it. So you must give it to me again."

The dove said, "I did not sing, I only cried."

Coyote bared his teeth. He said, "Do you prefer to be eaten?"

The dove quickly began to moan: "Hu-hu-huuu! Hu-hu-huuu! Ho-uuu, ho-uuu, ho-uuu!"

"Ah, now I have it," Coyote said, and once more he started for home. In his haste he slipped and tumbled into a gully. When he regained his footing, the song was gone. Again he had lost it. So he returned to the place where the dove was working.

"Your song is very slippery," he said. "It keeps getting away. Sing it again. This time I shall grasp it firmly. If I can't hold onto it this time I shall come and take you instead."

"I was not singing, I was crying," the dove said, but seeing Coyote's anger she repeated her moaning sounds.

And this time Coyote grasped the song firmly as he ran toward his home near Shipaulovi. When he was out of sight, the dove thought that it would be best for her to leave the kwakwi field. But before she left she found a stone that looked like a bird. She painted eyes on it and placed it where she had been working. Then she gathered up her kwakwi seeds and went away.

Coyote was tired from so much running back and forth. When he was almost home, he had to jump over a small ravine, but he misjudged the distance and fell. Now Coyote was truly angry, for the song had been lost again. He went back to the kwakwi field. He saw the stone that the dove had placed there. He saw the painted eyes looking at him.

"Now you have done it," he said. "There is no purpose in looking at me that way. I am a hunter. Therefore, I hunt." He leaped forward and his jaws snapped. But the stone bird was very hard. Coyote's teeth broke and his mouth began to bleed. "Hu-hu-huu!" he moaned. "Hu-hu-huuu! Ho-uuu, ho-uuu, ho-uuu!"

Just at that moment a crow alighted in the kwakwi field. He said, "Coyote, that is a beautiful song you are singing."

Coyote replied, "How stupid the crow people are that they can't tell the difference between singing and crying!"

Honwyma
and the Bear Fathers
of Tokoanave

❖

The people were living in the village of Oraibi. In a certain house the boy Honwyma lived with his parents and his little sister. He did all the things there are for boys to do. He worked in the fields, he hunted with his father, and he learned to make moccasins and arrows. But there was something else that he wanted, although he did not speak of it.

One day his father said to him, "I see you thinking. Why do you look into the distant sky as though you are searching for something there?"

Honwyma replied, "I want the knowledge of curing the sick. I want to be a medicine man."

His father said, "Such knowledge is hard to find. I do not have it."

Honwyma said, "Who then can teach me?"

And his father answered, "Who can say? Some men have been given the knowledge of medicine by the kachinas. Some have been taught by Spider Grandmother. Some have been taught by other medicine men. Be patient. If you were meant to know this thing it will come to you."

But Honwyma was not patient. One morning he took his bow and arrows and went down from the top of the mesa. He found antelope tracks and followed them. He saw an antelope. He pursued it and killed it with an arrow. He skinned it and put the hide to one side. He cut away the meat and put it aside. There were only bones remaining. He sat and studied the way the bones were shaped and how they fitted together. He took them apart and put them back in their right places. The sun began to go down, but he did not notice. It was only when a shadow fell on the ground beside him that he looked up. Standing there watching him was a man dressed in the ancient style. The man's hair hung down around his shoulders, and he wore a strip of woven cloth across his forehead. A black line was painted across the bridge of his nose and his cheekbones. This was the way the ancient people dressed.

The man asked, "Why do you sit there looking at bones? Is there something to be seen?"

Honwyma replied, "I am searching for the knowledge of medicine. I want to know how living things are made."

The man said, "Yes, I see that you are truly looking for the knowledge of things. Come with me. I will take you to a place where the knowledge may be found. It is far to the north. Let us begin."

They began walking. They traveled a great distance, and Honwyma became tired. The man said, "Wait here." He went behind a rock, and when he came back it was no longer in the form of a man, but of a large bear. He said, "Do not be afraid. I am one of the Bear People. Get on my back. I will carry you." So Honwyma got on the bear's back and rode.

The bear carried him northward toward the mountain known as Tokoanave. They arrived. When the bear came to an opening in the earth he stopped and Honwyma dismounted. The bear descended into the opening, and Honwyma followed him. Down below was a large kiva. Men were sitting there near the fireplace, talking and smoking. On the wall many bearskins were hanging. The man who had brought Honwyma to Tokoanave removed his bearskin and hung it on the wall with the others. Then he sat near the fire. A young girl brought food for Honwyma, and he sat down to eat. The men in the kiva passed a pipe back and forth. They watched Honwyma silently.

At last one of them spoke. He said, "We have been waiting for you to come."

Honwyma said, "You knew I was coming?"

The man answered, "Yes, that is why we are gathered here. You want to be a curer. We have heard your thoughts. We are going to give you the knowledge you are looking for. If you are ready to receive the knowledge you must become one of us, for the art of healing that we shall teach you belongs to the Bear People."

Honwyma said, "Yes, that is the way it will be."

The man went on, "When we have given you the gift of healing, this kiva at Tokoanave will be your home, and we shall be your fathers. When your life in Oraibi is over you will come and live with us here."

"Yes," Honwyma said, "let it be this way."

The man said, "Good. Let us start."

They brought out an owa cloth and spread it on the floor, and they instructed Honwyma to lie upon it. He lay down, and they covered him with a second owa cloth. They gathered around him, kneeling on the floor. They reached under the cloth that covered him and grasped his arms and legs. He felt great pain as they broke his bones, but he did not cry out. After the bones were broken the men set them back into place, making bear sounds as they worked. At last they said, "It is done." They removed the cloth covering and commanded Honwyma to get up. He was afraid to move, but he did so and felt no pain. He stood up. His bones were whole again.

One of the men said, "Now you are one of us. You have the power to heal. Return to your village. Use your power wisely. Do not boast. Do not proclaim your knowledge in public. In time people will know. Perform good deeds in Oraibi. But you must not say where you received the knowledge. When at last you feel death coming, leave word with your people that you are to be buried in the clothes that we shall give you. After death you will return here and remain forever among your Bear Fathers."

They dressed Honwyma in clothes like their own and made a black mark across his cheekbones and his nose. The man who had brought Honwyma to Tokoanave took his bearskin from the wall and went up the ladder. Outside the kiva he again became a bear. Honwyma mounted the bear's back. The bear carried him to the south, to the place where the boy had laid out the antelope bones, and there he left him.

Once more Honwyma hunted. He killed another antelope and brought the meat to his parents in Oraibi.

From that time on Honwyma lived in the kiva instead of in his parents' house. He came out only to eat with his family. Then he returned to the kiva. He told no one of his powers. He did not proclaim his knowledge of healing.

But one day his young sister fell from some high stone steps in the village. Honwyma heard her cry out and went up from the kiva. He found her lying motionless on the ground and carried her into the house. Her father said, "The breath of life is gone from her body. Go quickly to find a medicine man."

Honwyma answered, "Trust me. I shall take care of her."

He went outside and faced the north. He held up his hands and asked for help from his Bear Fathers at Tokoanave. He saw a light over the mountain and knew that he had been heard. He reentered the house. He placed his sister on an owa cloth, and he put another owa cloth over her. He reached under the covering. He made bear sounds as he worked. What he did his parents could not see. But soon there was a stirring under the cloth, and Honwyma removed it. His sister was breathing. She opened her eyes and stood up. She was well.

Honwyma's father asked, "Where did you get the knowledge?"

Honwyma answered, "It is a thing about which I cannot speak."

But from a distance a man of the village had seen Honwyma's

sister fall. He had said, "Surely the girl is dead." He had seen Honwyma carry her into the house, and he had seen Honwyma raise his hands toward Tokoanave. And afterwards he had seen the girl alive and well. He spoke of it to one person and another. People began coming to Honwyma to ask him to cure their illnesses. Whoever came for help, he helped them. And in this way his reputation spread even to the furthest villages.

Now, in the village of Polacca there were curers and men with special powers over fire, water, and the other elements of nature. They also heard of Honwyma, but they doubted what they heard. They said, "He is too young to understand such things. What people say about him must be false." Yet as time went on they heard more reports of Honwyma's cures. They were disturbed. They said to each other, "This boy must be a pretender. How can he know what it takes a lifetime to learn?" They decided that they would put Honwyma to a test. And so they sent word to medicine men in other villages that on a certain day they should meet in Polacca to demonstrate their powers. They also sent a messenger to invite Honwyma to come.

Before the day of the big meeting, however, Gogyeng Sowuti, Spider Grandmother, came to Honwyma to warn him. She said, "The medicine men are gathering in Polacca to test you. They intend to show that you are not a real healer. Do not hurry to show your powers. Let them show their powers first. Your turn will come later."

The day of the big meeting in Polacca came. Medicine men arrived from other villages. Honwyma was not among them. He was still in the kiva at Oraibi. So messengers were sent to get him. Arriving at the kiva in Oraibi, they said to him, "The gathering in Polacca has begun. The medicine men are there. They have heard of your knowledge. They are waiting for you to appear."

"Very well," Honwyma said. "I will come."

He put on the clothes given to him by his Bear Fathers and painted the black line on his cheeks. Then he went with the messengers to Polacca. As soon as he arrived, Honwyma was invited to display his powers, but he refused, saying, "No, I did not come for that purpose. I will watch the others."

So the men of a certain secret society entered the plaza to begin the demonstrations. They held their hands up toward the sun, and bolts of lightning flashed from their fingertips. A medicine man asked, "Can the boy from Oraibi do such a thing?"

But Honwyma said, "No, my powers are not like this."

One after another, groups of men entered the plaza to demonstrate their magical powers. Honwyma stood back. He observed, but he said nothing. Time after time he was invited to exhibit his knowledge, but he said, "No, not yet. A time will come for it."

The medicine men began to say to each other, "It is just as we thought. The boy is a fraud."

And now a group of men came forward to demonstrate their knowledge of how to bring the dead back to life. Singing their ritual song, they climbed to the roof of the highest house in the village. To one side of the house was a deep ravine filled with rocks. Still singing, they took hold of one of their men and threw him into the ravine. He fell upon the rocks and lay there without moving. They left him, the breath of life gone from his body, and went down from the roof and danced in the plaza. After a while they descended into their kiva to prepare medicine to bring him back to life. They were gone a long time, and when they emerged from the kiva one of the men carried the medicine in a bowl. But as they approached the plaza he fell, breaking the bowl and scattering the medicine on the ground. So they had to return to the kiva and begin all over. They prepared medicine a second time. They were gone a long while. At last they came out of the kiva again, but by this time the body of the man who had been thrown on the rocks was cold. They carried him to the plaza and laid him on an owa cloth, and placed another owa cloth over him. Then four of the men put their hands under the cover and began to do their work. But nothing happened, and after a while another group of four took over the task. They were older men who had stronger powers. Nothing happened. Another group tried, and then still another, but the body remained without life. The people said, "Let the boy from Oraibi try."

Honwyma said, "I never boasted of my powers. I never spoke of them. It was you who spoke of the matter. You brought me here to test me, though I had no thought of such a thing. You people, now after the body of this man has already grown cold you ask me to try to bring life back to him. Very well, I will try."

He turned his face toward the north, in the direction of Tokoanave. He raised his hands, asking for help from his Bear Fathers. Then he kneeled by the body and placed his hands under the owa covering. As he worked he made bear sounds in his throat. Time passed. Some people said, "See, the boy from Oraibi can do nothing." But Honwyma did not hear. He went on working, and at last he removed his hands from under the owa cloth. The other medicine men said, "He does not have the power of medicine."

Honwyma stood up. He said, "Remove the owa cloth."

They removed it. The man lay there. There was sweat on his skin and he was breathing. He opened his eyes. He sat up.

The people who had come to witness the tests of power exclaimed, "What the others failed at, Honwyma has done! He has brought this man back to life!" And by their silence, the medicine men at Polacca acknowledged Honwyma's victory over death.

Honwyma returned to Oraibi. Once more he went into the kiva, and there he lived in the days that followed. It was there that people always found him when someone was sick and needed help. Time went on. He grew older, but he did not take a wife as other young men did. He devoted himself to healing. Each day when it was time to eat, his sister came into the kiva to call him to the house. He would go up, eat, and then return to the kiva.

One day it seemed to him that he heard the voices of his Bear Fathers, and he understood that his time had come to prepare for the journey to Tokoanave. He showed his sister the clothes he was to be dressed in. Then he lay down to wait. In the morning when Honwyma's sister came to call him for the first meal of the day she found him lying there. Death had taken him. They carried him from the kiva into the house. They dressed him in the clothes he was supposed to wear, and they marked his cheeks with the black line worn by the ancient ones. They buried him.

Thus it was that Honwyma returned to Tokoanave to live with the Bear Fathers who had given him the power to cure.

Two Friends, Coyote and Bull Snake, Exchange Visits

❖

The bull snake and Coyote were friends. The bull snake lived in his kiva on the mesa, and Coyote lived in his kiva near Homolovi. One time the bull snake went on a trip to visit Coyote. He arrived at Homolovi and went a little beyond until he came to Coyote's place.

Standing at the entrance to the kiva, he called out, as was the custom, "Ha'u!"

Looking up, Coyote saw his friend and answered, "Kawawatamuy! Enter and be welcome!"

The bull snake entered. He went down the ladder into the kiva, pulling his long tail behind him. He coiled next to the fireplace. More and more of his tail followed him, and as he coiled himself he began to fill up the kiva. Coyote went up the ladder a little to make room for his guest. But there was still more of the bull snake to come in, and Coyote went further up the ladder. When at last the bull snake was entirely in, Coyote found himself outside, looking down through the opening.

"How good it is to be with a friend," the bull snake said.

"Yes, it is good," Coyote said from above. "Let us smoke a pipe, let us talk."

They smoked. They talked. Inside the kiva the bull snake was warm and comfortable. Outside, Coyote felt the north wind and was cold.

"Yes," the bull snake said, "what is better than to sit together this way?"

"Yes, yes," Coyote said, "it is truly so." But he was cold, and he was angry that he had to sit outside while the bull snake was so comfortable near the fire.

The night passed, and the bull snake departed. Coyote was still angry about what had happened. He decided to return the visit. But first he went out to the place where the cedar trees grew. He stripped bark from the trees. He pounded the bark to make it soft. Then he fashioned it into a long tail. He pulled some hairs out of his skin and stuck them to the cedar-bark tail with tree gum. And on a certain day Coyote fastened the cedar-bark tail behind him and went north to visit the bull snake. He came to the spring at Toreva, passed it, and arrived at the bull snake's kiva.

From the entrance he called out, "Ha'u!"

From inside, the bull snake answered, "Kawawatamuy! Enter and be welcome!"

Coyote went down the ladder, pulling his cedar-bark tail behind him. He walked around in a circle, coiling his tail on the floor. As more and more tail entered, the bull snake moved up the ladder to make room. In the end, Coyote's tail filled the kiva, and the bull snake had to sit outside.

"How good it is to be with a friend," Coyote said. "Let us smoke a pipe. Let us talk."

They smoked. They talked. Coyote was warm near the fire, but outside the bull snake felt the north wind. He shivered.

He said, "My friend, you have grown somewhat."

"Yes, it is so," Coyote replied. "That is the way it is with all living things."

The bull snake said no more about Coyote's long tail, remembering how it was when he visited Coyote at Homolovi. But he kept thinking, "Now how can it be? His tail was not so long the last time we met." When at last Coyote decided to leave, the bull snake looked closely at the tail as it came up the ladder. And as Coyote made room for him he descended into the kiva. Some of the cedar-bark tail was still there. The bull snake took the very end of it and put it in the fire, and soon it began to smoke, and it burst into flame. The burning tail went up the ladder and disappeared from the kiva.

Coyote went southward toward Homolovi. He was very pleased with the memory of the bull snake sitting in the wind all night while he himself was warm. As he walked, thinking this way, his smoldering tail set the dry grass afire. Coyote turned and saw the burning grass. He began to run. Wherever the tail touched the grass it made new fire. He ran faster and faster. He went through a cornfield and set it ablaze. He was not yet halfway to Homolovi. He turned toward the west to find water.

He ran through a patch of timber and started a forest fire. Wherever he passed, he left fire behind. He came to the Little Colorado River and leaped into it. When the fire reached the river it stopped.

But Coyote did not stop. He crossed the river and went on. It is said that the trail that Coyote made can still be seen, for in some places there are the charred trees that remain from the forest fire, and elsewhere there are the marks left by his cedar-bark tail in the sand.

The Foot Racers
of Payupki
❖

In the old days, as is known, there were two villages, one named Payupki and the other Tikuvi. Payupki was the smaller and Tikuvi the larger. In Tikuvi there were many good foot racers, but in Payupki there were few.

One day the chief of Payupki saw the people of Tikuvi going out to their running grounds to have races. He sent for a certain boy in his village. He said to him, "The people of Tikuvi are racing today. I would like to know how good their runners are. You are the best runner we have in Payupki. Go down and join them. Run with them. Let me know what you learn."

The boy runner of Payupki went to the Tikuvi races. The people welcomed him and invited him to join the contest. So he ran in the long race. The best runners of Tikuvi were in it. At first the boy from Payupki was far behind. But as the race went on, he moved forward. There were two runners ahead of him. Then there was only one. He desired to win, but he remembered that the chief had told him only to get information about the Tikuvi runners. So he allowed the Tikuvi runner to finish first. When the racing was over, the Payupki boy returned home.

He said to the chief, "I went to the running grounds. I joined in the long race. Though I finished second, I believe I could have won. But I did not press on."

The chief answered, "You have told me what I wanted to know. Some day we shall run against Tikuvi. Meanwhile, train yourself and make your legs grow strong."

So the boy trained himself. Every day he went running. He ran across the mesa, he ran on the low ground, he ran in the hills. He felt himself grow stronger. And one day the chief of Tikuvi came to Payupki. He found the chief of Payupki down in the kiva. He entered. They greeted one another, and they smoked together. When the tobacco was consumed, the chief of Payupki put the pipe away. He said, "We are glad you have come. What is in your mind?"

The chief of Tikuvi answered, "I came to tell you that four days from now my village will have a racing festival. We would like you to come with your best runners. Bring whatever you wish for betting. We shall do the same."

The chief of Payupki said, "We are a small village. We have only one good runner here, the one you know about. We shall bring him."

It was arranged.

The night before the races were to take place, the men of Tikuvi went into their kiva to discuss the contest.

One of them said, "The boy from Payupki may beat our runners. We may lose whatever we bet."

Another said, "You forget that he ran against us before and did not win. Why should we be concerned?"

They argued this way back and forth, and decided at last that there was nothing to fear from Payupki's single runner. While they sat there talking, Spider Grandmother came with her medicine bag. She descended to the first level of the kiva, and as she started down toward the lower level the men shouted at her, "Go away, Grandmother."

She stopped, saying, "I have come to give help to our runners. I have brought medicine to put on them."

They replied, "Go away, Grandmother. Our runners don't need your help."

She said, "When you are in trouble you send for me, but now you say, 'We don't need you, Grandmother, go away.' It is you who have said it. Therefore, I shall leave."

She climbed the ladder and went out of the kiva. She went to her house on the edge of Tikuvi and gathered her things together. Then she left Tikuvi and went across to the village of Payupki.

When she arrived in Payupki the people welcomed her and took her to the kiva where the men of the village were discussing the next day's contest. Spider Grandmother began to go down the ladder. Seeing her coming, the men called out, "Come down, Grandmother! Come down!" She sat with them. The chief gave her a pipe to smoke. She smoked energetically. She blew great clouds of smoke from her mouth. The men smiled, thinking, "Spider Grandmother is old. She takes in too much smoke. In a few minutes she will become dizzy and fall over." But Spider Grandmother did not fall over. She blew out more clouds of smoke, and after the tobacco was finished she returned the pipe to the chief.

He said to her, "You are welcome here. Why have you come?"

She replied, "I lived in Tikuvi. I went to the kiva to give help to their runners who will race tomorrow. But the men laughed at me. They said, 'Go away, old woman.' So I left Tikuvi. I have come to your village, and now I will help your runner."

She took a bowl from her bag. She put a magic powder in it. She added water and made medicine. She said, "This is to protect your runner against sorcery." They brought Payupki's boy runner into the kiva. Spider Grandmother rubbed the medicine on his legs.

Then she said, "In Tikuvi they will sit up all night celebrating. Here in Payupki we should sleep."

The chief said, "Spider Grandmother speaks wisely. Let us sleep."

The people found a room in the village for Spider Grandmother. They built a fire in it to warm her. They brought blankets for her. Then the village of Payupki slept.

The next morning the men and boys gathered and went to the Tikuvi racing grounds.

"Where are the runners?" the chief of Tikuvi asked.

The best runners of Tikuvi came forward. The boy runner of

Payupki came forward. The men of the two villages began to make bets. They bet whatever things they had brought—moccasins, belts, shawls, kilts, even bows and arrows. The first race began. The boy from Payupki won. The second race began. The boy from Payupki won. He ran against Tikuvi's fastest runners and won every race. When it was over, the men of Payupki collected the things they had won from the men of Tikuvi and carried them home. They gave some of their winnings to Spider Grandmother, and she was contented.

The chief of Payupki sent for the boy runner. He said, "Now you must learn to run as you have never run before. The people of Tikuvi are angry. They will come again with another challenge, and we must be ready."

The boy worked hard to become a better runner. Every morning at dawn he went out to run. One day his sister said to him, "I saw you running today, but your feet were slow."

He replied, "Didn't I win over the runners of Tikuvi?"

She said, "Nevertheless, tomorrow I will show you about running."

The next day she went with him to the running place. He said, "Go ahead of me. Stand beyond the large rock where the cottonwood tree is. I shall start from here."

The girl said, "I do not need to start ahead of you."

He answered, "Do as I say. When we start running, go to the sand hole in the east, then return."

So his sister went ahead to the large rock, and they began. The boy was surprised. Instead of closing the distance between them, he fell further behind. When his sister reached the sand hole, he was still a long way off. She passed him coming back, saying, "Run, brother, run!" By the time he made his turn around the sand hole she was far away. When he was halfway back, she had already finished. He returned to the village. There he found his sister busy grinding corn.

He asked, "Aren't you too tired to grind corn?"

"No," she said, "it was nothing."

Again the next day they went out to run together. This time they started from the same place. But soon the girl was far in front. She went around the sand hole and passed her brother going the other way. She taunted him, saying, "Run, brother, run!" He could not catch her. She finished and went on to the village. He arrived at his house. He saw his sister grinding corn.

He asked, "Sister, aren't you too tired to do that?"

She said, "No, the running was nothing."

The following day they went again to the running place. The girl said, "I shall start from here. You go ahead and begin at the large rock where the cottonwood tree is."

He went ahead, wondering whether even this advantage would help him. They began. Before he reached the sand hole, his sister has passed him. She left him far behind, finished, and went on to the village. The boy arrived. He went to the chief's house. He said, "I am not the fastest runner in Payupki. My sister is the fastest." The chief pondered on it.

In time the chief of Tikuvi came again to visit with the chief of Payupki. They sat in the kiva and smoked. At last the chief of

Tikuvi said, "We are having races four days from now. Bring your best runner. He will race against our young men."

The chief of Payupki answered, "It is agreed. We shall come. But now our best runner is a girl." The chief of Tikuvi listened. They talked, and then he went home to Tikuvi where he told the people what he had learned.

The night before the race came, and the men of Tikuvi went to the kiva to make plans. Because they had been beaten before, they knew that if they were to win this time, they would have to use sorcery. They sent a messenger to get Spider Grandmother, but he came back without her, saying, "She is not there. Her house is empty. It looks as if no one lives there now." But they had other people with the knowledge of sorcery, and they devised a plan to win the contest.

In the kiva at Payupki, also, there was planning. Spider Grandmother rubbed the legs of the girl runner with her medicine. She said, "The people of Tikuvi are bad-hearted. They intend to win the contest by sorcery. So when the girl runs I will take on my other form and become a spider. I will sit on her ear and tell her what to do."

The night passed, and the day of the race came. Everyone gathered at the Tikuvi racing grounds. This time not only the men of Payupki came, but the women also, because it was a girl who was going to represent the village. People bet whatever they had brought—moccasins, bows, belts, turquoise beads, shawls, even pots and grinding stones. The girl from Payupki tucked up her skirt under her belt and prepared to run. The first

race began, it ended. The girl from Payupki won. The people of
Tikuvi paid their debt to the people of Payupki. The second race
was run. The Payupki girl finished first. Again the people of
Tikuvi paid what they owed. The girl won the third race, and the
fourth. By now the people of Tikuvi had lost everything they had
brought to bet on the contest.

It was time for the last race to start. The Payupki men wanted
the betting to go on. The Tikuvi men said, "We have nothing
more." They were sullen. They were ready to leave. But the
Tikuvi women looked at the piles of things the Payupki people
had won. They said, "We want to go on with the betting. We
have no more things to put up. But we will do it this way. If our
runner wins, all those things in the piles will belong to us, the
things that were ours and the things that are yours. If your runner
wins, all the women of our village will belong to you. We will go
to Payupki and become the wives of Payupki men." The Tikuvi
men did not like it. They discussed it. At last, because they
planned to use sorcery to win the final race, they decided to take
a chance. They felt certain of victory. They agreed. And the
people of Payupki also agreed.

So the final race began, and Spider Grandmother changed
herself into a spider and sat on the Payupki girl's ear. At first the
girl and the boy runner of Tikuvi ran together, neither one
ahead and neither one behind. But after a while the girl took
the lead. Spider Grandmother urged her on, saying in her ear,
"Run, daughter, run!" Suddenly there was a whirring sound, and
a white dove flew past them. Spider Grandmother said, "You

see what they are doing? They have transformed the boy into a bird."

The dove was far ahead when they reached the turning place. So Spider Grandmother called out to a hawk that was sitting on a tall rock on top of the mesa. The hawk swooped down from its perch and struck the dove. The dove fell to the ground and fluttered there while the girl runner passed him. But after a while they heard the whirring sound again, and once more the dove was in the lead. Again Spider Grandmother called on the hawk to strike, and again it came down and knocked the dove to the ground. The girl, with Spider Grandmother on her ear, took the lead. When they were almost in sight of the finishing place, the dove passed them for the third time. Once more Spider Grandmother called the hawk. Again it came and struck the dove down. Now the girl runner of Payupki ran swiftly and ended the race. The people of her village applauded her as she finished. But the people of Tikuvi were silent. The Tikuvi men were sour and angry, for they had lost their women. They spoke black words at their runner when he arrived.

The Payupki people took up all their winnings, they took the Tikuvi women, and they went home and celebrated their victory, not forgetting to give presents to Spider Grandmother. As for the men of Tikuvi, after they got home they tried to do all the things the women used to do for them, but they did things badly. As time went on they became more and more angry over what had happened to them. At last they decided to go to Payupki and

fight. They made bows. They made arrows. They prepared for battle.

Spider Grandmother heard about the happenings, and she called the people of Payupki to the kiva. She said, "In Tikuvi they are preparing for war. They are busy smoothing their arrows and bending juniper saplings to make bows. They plan to come at night when we are sleeping or when we are inside the kiva. They plan to kill all the men and to take all the women to Tikuvi. In Tikuvi there are many men, while in Payupki there are few. Therefore, there is only one thing to do. We must leave this village and go to another place where we will be safe. I know of such a place in the east, at the edge of flowing water. I will guide you to it."

The people talked it over. They agreed with Spider Grandmother. They prepared to leave at once. As the first gray light of dawn came, the men and the boys went out and rounded up all their cattle and horses and placed them in a corral. The women prepared food for them to carry. Spider Grandmother gave them directions. "Go east to the wall of the mesa," she said. "Descend by the trail, and go on until you reach the deep canyon. Take the cattle through the canyon until you reach the springs. There the cattle may drink. After that, continue on for four days. The women will follow you." The men left, driving the cattle ahead of them. They followed Spider Grandmother's directions. They passed the village of Awatovi. They went on. They found the watering place in the canyon and continued the journey to the east.

After the men had left Payupki, the women prepared for their journey. They saved what they could from their houses. They packed food, clothing, pots, and grinding stones. They put the baskets on their backs, bracing them with straps around their foreheads. The loads were very heavy. Spider Grandmother spoke, saying, "With such loads as these we shall never get where we are going. Therefore, something must be left behind." She brought out a large jar and placed it on the ground. She said, "We are going far. We cannot carry everything. We must take only what we need. Let us put everything else in this jar." So everything that was not necessary for life was placed in the large jar, including their turquoise jewelry. They sealed the jar and buried it in the ground. Then they started east, following the tracks of the men. Some days later they caught up with the men, who were waiting for them. There they rested in a temporary camp until Spider Grandmother told them it was time to move again.

Once more they went eastward. They had not been traveling long when they saw a stranger coming from the other direction. He also was driving cattle before him. The stranger stopped and spoke to the chief of Payupki, but the chief could not understand him. Spider Grandmother came. She understood all languages. She listened to the man and said, "This man is a Castilla. He wants to gamble with us."

The chief asked, "What kind of game does he want to play?"

"He has cattle, we have cattle," Spider Grandmother said. "He wants to bet his cattle against ours."

"No," the chief said, "that is not possible. We have come too far to take such a risk. These cattle are all that we have left."

"Unless we gamble," Spider Grandmother said, "he will not let us pass."

"Can he prevent us?" the chief asked.

"Yes," Spider Grandmother answered, "he carries a magic killing stick."

"Very well," the chief said. "Since we have no choice, we will do it. What is the contest?"

The Castilla pointed to a dead tree standing in the distance. Spider Grandmother said, "It is this way: He will shoot his weapon at the tree. One of our men will shoot at the tree. Whoever splits the tree wins the contest."

The chief called the best bowman of Payupki to come forward. He had strong arms and a thick hunting bow. The chief said, "You will compete for us. May your arrow fly straight and hard, for all of our cattle depend on it."

The Castilla tried first. He raised his magic stick and pointed it at the dead tree. There was a loud noise, and black smoke came out of the end of the stick, but the tree remained as it was. Now it was the turn of the Payupki bowman. Spider Grandmother asked the Payupki chief to name the best medicine man in the village. The chief named him, and Spider Grandmother told him to come and stand with the bowman. He came and stood there. Spider Grandmother instructed him what to do.

As the bowman placed his arrow against the bowstring, the medicine man called out: "Place your arrow in the bow!" Instantly a dark storm cloud formed overhead. As the bowman pulled back his bowstring, the medicine man called out: "The bow is bent!" And when he said this, the storm cloud grew larger. As the bowman released the arrow, the medicine man called out: "The arrow flies!" There was a loud clap of thunder and a bolt of lightning came down from the sky. For a moment the dead tree glowed as though it were on fire. Then it shattered and fell in many pieces. The people went to where the tree had stood. They saw the arrow sticking in a fragment of the wood. They looked at the Castilla. He turned his eyes away, thinking that he would not pay the bet. But he looked again at the shattered tree and at the dark storm cloud hovering overhead.

At last he said, "You have won. Never before have I seen such a thing. Take my cattle."

So the people of Payupki took his cattle, and now their herd was much larger than before. They went on to the east. They traveled many days, and they arrived at the place Spider Grandmother had chosen for them at the edge of the running water. They built a new village there, just a little south of a place called Sioki, and they gave it the name of their old village, Payupki.

The old village that they abandoned in fear of the men of Tikuvi, you can still see its ruins. It was built in ancient times, and then it was left behind. This is the story of how it happened.

Why the Salt
Is Far Away

❖

One day, as they often did, the twins Pokanghoya and Polong-ahoya went out to play nahoydadatsya. Hitting the ball with their sticks, they went wherever the game led them, paying no attention to distance or direction. They came to a wide field of tall grass, and as they could not play with their ball there, they stopped. There was a breeze, and it made the grass sway back and forth. The swaying grass made a swishing sound.

"Listen," Pokanghoya said. "The grass is singing. It is going 'sh, sh, sh,' like that."

"I hear it," Polongahoya said. "See, it is also dancing. It goes this way, then that way, then this way, then that way."

"Yes," Pokanghoya said, "it is singing and dancing."

The two boys stood for a long while watching the grass move and listening to the sound as it swayed. Afterwards they returned home, hitting their nahoydadatsya ball as they traveled.

Spider Grandmother was waiting for them. She said, "Where have you been? It is late."

The boys said, "We have been to the dance."

Spider Grandmother said, "I did not hear that there was to be a dance anywhere."

"Oh, yes," Pokanghoya said, "there was a dance. They sang 'sh, sh, sh,' like that."

Polongahoya said, "Yes, and they danced this way and that way." He bent forward and backward to show Spider Grandmother the way it was.

Pokanghoya said, "The dancers wore tassels in their hair."

Polongahoya said, "Yes, it was down there in the big fields south of the mesa."

Spider Grandmother said, "You boys, what are you thinking of? You have been watching the grass in the wind. That was no dance. If you really want to see a dance, go to Shongopovi four days from now. You will see the women doing the Lalakon Dance. They will be giving out coiled basket trays. There will be real singing. The people will not just say 'sh, sh, sh,' like the grass."

So on the fourth day the two boys took their ball and their playing sticks and started out for Shongopovi. They played as they went, and they followed their ball into gullies and mud-holes, never stopping, so that when they arrived at Shongopovi they were very dirty. The dancing was already going on. The women were dancing with their coiled basket trays in their hands, and from time to time they threw the trays in the air for the men to catch. Pokanghoya and Polongahoya tried to catch the trays, but they could not do it because they were pushed aside by the men. And now some of the people of Shongopovi

invited strangers in the village to come into their houses and eat.
But the two boys were so dirty that no one wanted them. They
were ignored. They were very hungry because they had not
eaten anything since early morning. And they became angry at
the way they were being treated.

Polongahoya said, "Let us go home. These people don't per-
mit us to catch the coiled trays. They do not offer us anything
to eat."

Pokanghoya said, "Yes, let us go. But first let us each get a
coiled tray."

So they rushed in where the dance was still going on, and each
of them grabbed a tray. Then they ran out of the village and went
home.

Spider Grandmother greeted them. She asked, "Did you see
the dancing in Shongopovi?"

They said, "We saw it, but the people were not generous.
They would not let us catch the coiled basket trays. And no one
gave us food. We are very hungry."

Spider Grandmother put out food for them. They ate.

Then they said, "The people did not act well toward us. They
treated us badly. Therefore, we shall punish them."

Now all the places where the people got their salt in those
days belonged to Pokanghoya and Polongahoya. It was the
twins who had created the salt beds and made salt available to
the people. As it was, the people had to walk a distance to the
nearest salt bed. When Pokanghoya and Polongahoya had finished eating, they went to that place and gathered up the salt and

took it farther away, leaving it in a rocky spot that was very hard to get at.

Later the people of the villages went to the place where they usually found their salt, but there was hardly any salt left, only what the brothers had spilled. So they had to look elsewhere. In time they found the rocky place where the brothers had taken the salt, but it was very far away. Ever since then the people have had to travel a great distance to get their salt. The reason is that when Pokanghoya and Polongahoya went to the Lalakon Dance at Shongopovi they were badly treated.

How the Village
of Pivanhonkapi
Perished

❖

It is said that northwest of Oraibi in ancient times there was a village called Pivanhonkapi. Life was good there. The springs were full of water and food was plentiful. But Pivanhonkapi perished suddenly and became a ruin, so the old people say, and this is how it came to be.

Because life was so good to them the people of the village lost their gratitude for the many kindnesses of nature. The young forgot to respect the old, and the old forgot respect for the kachinas who brought rain and bountiful crops of corn. Whereas in earlier times men sat in the kivas at night and discussed the forces and mysteries of life, now the kivas were used only for playing games and exchanging gossip. Instead of making prayer sticks the men made totolospi sticks to gamble with, and the women came into the kivas to gamble with the men. Even the wife of the chief forgot her duties and went to the kivas to join in the gossip and games. When her children cried, the chief himself had to go after her and bring her home to take care of them. Those who were weavers forgot to do their weaving, and those

114

who made pots baked them carelessly. Women forgot to make piki bread for the festivals, and men forgot to weed their fields. The people of Pivanhonkapi forgot the Hopi way of life.

The chief of the village brooded on the evils that had come among his people. He decided that something must be done. Now, in a certain place not far away lived the Yayaponcha people. The Yayaponchas were feared. They had long and unkempt hair, and they were known to be sorcerers with special powers over the forces of nature. They could make the north wind blow, call down destructive storms, make the lightning strike, and control fire. The chief of Pivanhonkapi went to the place where the Yayaponchas lived. They received him and took him into their kiva. They called a council of the old men. When they were all gathered, the Pivanhonkapi chief spoke, saying, "I have come to speak with you about a certain matter."

They replied, "You are welcome to speak of it."

He said, "The spirit of my village is sick. The people have become dark-hearted. They care nothing for virtue. They behave badly. Respect for things that deserve respect has vanished. Reverence for the things our ancestors taught us has disappeared. Day after day and night after night the people gamble in the kivas. Mothers neglect their children, and young men laugh at the old. Men forget who their wives are, and women forget who their husbands are. This evil must come to an end. Therefore, I wish to call down the fury of nature to bring judgment on Pivanhonkapi."

The Yayaponcha people listened. They discussed what they

had heard. And finally their leader said, "Yes, we will help you bring judgment. But what shall it be? Shall it be water, or storm, or lightning, or wind, or fire?"

The chief of Pivanhonkapi pondered on it. Then he said, "Let it be fire."

It was agreed that in four days there would be a dance at Pivanhonkapi and that the Yayaponchas would come to take part. The chief departed. On his way home he stopped at the village of Huckovi. To the chief of Huckovi, who was his friend, he told the secret that a judgment by fire was to be made on the people of Pivanhonkapi, and he invited him to come to the dance.

The day of the festivities came. Kachinas danced in the plaza. Each group of kachinas performed its own dance and its own songs. One group of dancers departed from the plaza, another appeared. The dancing went on all day. The last to appear were the Yayaponchas. Four of them carried prayer offerings of corn-meal, and on top of each prayer offering was a spark of fire. As the Yayaponchas danced, they sang. The Pivanhonkapi people heard the words:

> *"Houses will be enveloped in a red cloud*
> *Coming from the south,*
> *Wrapping itself around one village and another.*
> *Here it will be at last."*

The people of Pivanhonkapi did not understand the meaning of the words, but they were alarmed because the Yayaponchas seemed to speak of some great mystery.

When the dance came to an end, the prayer offerings, each with its spark of fire, were distributed. The Pivanhonkapi chief received one, and he placed it in his house. The chief of Huckovi received one, which he carried back to his village. The chief of the Yayaponchas kept one, which he took home with him. And the fourth prayer offering with its spark of fire was carried by a runner to the distant southern sacred peaks now known as the San Francisco Mountains. The runner left the prayer offering there and went away.

The day of the dance ended in Pivanhonkapi, and the people soon began to forget. They forgot their alarm over the Yayaponcha song that had spoken of a red cloud coming from the south. They forgot the prayer offerings and the kachinas. And they went back to gambling in the kivas. But the next night a few people who were not in the kivas noticed a red glow in the sky above the San Francisco Mountains. They called down into the kivas to tell what they had seen, but what they said aroused no interest there. The next night it seemed as though the mountains themselves were afire, and again the news was carried to the kivas, and again the people down below were too busy to listen. On the third night the whole southern sky was alight, resembling an enormous red cloud. The gamblers only laughed when the news was brought to them. By the fourth day the great fire had reached the foot of the mesa. The people came out of the kivas to see what was happening. They began to cry out. They ran this way and that, not knowing what to do. Soon they could see that the village of Huckovi was being swallowed in flames. As

the fire approached Pivanhonkapi, the villagers fled for their
lives.

Only a few people of Huckovi and Pivanhonkapi escaped.
Most of them died. The chief of Pivanhonkapi and the chief of
Huckovi also perished. There was nothing left of the two villages but ruins. The proof of what happened lies there today in
the smoke-blackened stones and the bits of pottery that cover
the ground where the villages once stood.

The ancient village of Oraibi lay directly in the path of the
great fire, yet Oraibi was not destroyed, and this is how it
came to be. When the people of Oraibi saw the flames coming in
the south they went to their chief with the news. He climbed to
the highest roof to see for himself. Then he went to the place
where Gogyeng Sowuti, Spider Grandmother, had her kiva at
the edge of the mesa.

"The fire coming from the south is destroying everything," he
said to Spider Grandmother. "Soon it will reach Oraibi. How can
I save my people?"

Spider Grandmother told him to make two arrows decorated
with the feathers of a bluebird. This he did. Spider Grandmother
took him to a spot west of the village and said, "Put an arrow
here." He pressed the point of the arrow into the ground. Spider
Grandmother took him to another spot east of the village and
said, "Put the other arrow here." He pressed the point of the
second arrow into the ground. Then Spider Grandmother spun a
web between the two arrows, and when it was finished she
moistened the web with water. The fire came. It reached the web

but it could not pass, so it turned and went another way, leaving Oraibi unharmed. Thus Oraibi was saved from destruction.

As for the Yayaponchas whose songs and prayer offerings created the fire, they are no longer there on the mesa. The old people say that the Yayaponchas scattered, in time, some going to live with the Walpi people, some going to live in Oraibi. It is said that the Yayaponchas eventually lost their special powers over the elements of nature. They are no longer seen in Hopi country, and it is only the ancient tales that speak of them.

The Sun Callers

❖

At a certain place north of Oraibi, Coyote was living there, and a little beyond that the rooster was living. Now, it was in the dark of the night, and Coyote was going around looking for something to eat. There in the darkness he met the rooster, who was sitting on a high rock. He greeted the rooster, saying, "Ha'u," and the rooster greeted Coyote the same way.

Coyote said, "What are you doing there? Why are you not at home this time of the night?"

The rooster said, "I have work to do. I have to make the sun rise."

Coyote said, "You take yourself too seriously. Anyone can make the sun rise."

The rooster answered, "No, indeed, it is only I who can do it."

Coyote said, "On the contrary, I am the one who has the power to make the sun come up."

"Let us have a test," the rooster said. "Whoever makes the sun appear, he shall be acknowledged as the Sun Caller."

"That is good," Coyote said. "I will try first."

He sat back on his haunches, pointed his nose toward the sky, and howled to summon the sun. He went on doing this until he was breathless, but the sky remained as black as ever.

"Enough," the rooster said. "Now I will try." He stretched his neck, flapped his wings, and crowed. Once, twice, several times he crowed, but still the night was black.

Coyote said, "Now it is my turn," and again he howled until he was breathless, but around them there was still nothing but darkness.

The rooster said, "You are wasting your time. I will show you how it is done." He stretched his neck, flapped his wings, and crowed. Again and again he called the sun, but nothing happened.

"Now pay attention," Coyote said. "This is the way to do it." He put his nose up and howled with great feeling, telling the sun it was time to appear. But everything was still the same, and there was only darkness all around them.

They went on this way, taking turns all through the night. And one time after the rooster crowed, things were a little lighter. "You see," the rooster said, "I am beginning to do it."

Then Coyote tried again, and things were a little lighter still. Coyote said, "It is quite clear that I did better than you."

But the sun had not appeared, and the rooster tried once more. He filled his lungs with air, stretched his neck, flapped his wings, and crowed mightily. And as he did so, the red edge of the sun appeared over the horizon.

"My friend," the rooster said, "you can judge for yourself. As anyone can see, it was I who brought the sun up from down below."

Coyote said, "Yes, I acknowledge it. You have powerful medicine. You are the Sun Caller."

Coyote went away. But he kept thinking, "I almost did it. Once when I called, the night grew a little lighter. Perhaps with practice I can do it." And even to this time, every so often in the night you can hear Coyote trying again to make the sun rise. But the rooster, he is the one that really does it. And because his work goes on and on without ever ending, he has grown hoarse. You can hear it for yourself.

The Journey to
the Land of
the Dead

❖

In the village of Oraibi, living alone in a certain house near the rim of the mesa, there was a young widow. Many men had sought her for a wife, but she did not want any of them. Sometimes a young man would come and look through the small window in the side of her house and watch her working. He would try to make conversation with her, but she would not look up from her corn grinding, so he would go away. Many young men came to talk with her this way, thinking, "I will make her my wife," but she gave none of them any encouragement.

It happened one time that a young man named Talahoyama passed her in the village. He turned to watch her. Though he said nothing, the young woman thought she heard him speak. She also turned for a moment. Then she went on. Talahoyama could not get her from his mind. And so one day he went to the window of her house and watched her grinding corn. After a while she said, "Why are you standing there?"

He answered, "I am merely watching you grind corn."

She said, "Have you never before seen a woman grinding corn?"

He answered, "Other women, yes. But you, this is the first time I have seen you doing it."

In time he went away, but the next day he came again. Day after day he returned, and after a while the young woman came to expect him. She would say to herself, "Will he come today?" Or, "He should have been here before now." One day he found her making piki.

She said, "Have you never before seen a woman making piki?"

He replied, "Yes, I have seen it."

She said, "You are not talkative like other men."

"No," he said, "I do not want to disturb you."

She laughed and came to the window. He stayed for a long while that day. They became friends. It went on this way, and at last they were married.

Now, among the other men who had courted the young widow, there were some who belonged to a society of sorcerers. They saw the way things were going, and when the woman married Talahoyama, they became angry. They met in their kiva and discussed the matter. "I was there many times," one of them said, "but she would not speak to me." Another said, "Yes, it was that way with me also. She turned me away." Another said, "I, too, approached her, but she rejected me." It was agreed among the sorcerers that the woman would have to leave Talahoyama. So one of them put on his mask and painted his arms and legs and went to the house where Talahoyama and his wife were living. He entered and stood by the wall in the shadows.

He said, "Some of our people came to this woman's house. They wanted to marry her, but she refused them. We cannot leave it this way." To Talahoyama's wife the man said, "You must leave him. One of our people will marry you."

Talahoyama answered, "She is my wife. Therefore we shall live together."

His wife said, "Yes, that is the way it is."

The sorcerer said, "You have spoken badly. And now, for this reason, you must gamble for your lives."

They asked, "What is the contest?"

"We shall play the sleeping game," the sorcerer said. "We have powerful medicine to make you sleep. If either of you sleeps for even a moment during the next four nights and days, he will die. If both of you sleep, both die." And after saying this he went out and disappeared in the night.

Talahoyama said, "Very well. For four nights and days we shall not sleep."

His wife said, "Yes, we shall not sleep."

Instead of lying down that night they sat near their fire and talked. If Talahoyama saw his wife getting sleepy, he gave her things to do. He said, "Bring more fuel to put on the fire," or, "I am thirsty. Please bring me water."

And if she thought her husband was about to close his eyes, she said, "Your hunting bow needs restringing," or, "Your shield has a hole in it. It should be repaired."

In this way they went through the night without sleeping, and when day came they arose and did the things that are done in the daylight hours.

The second night was harder than the first, and the third night was harder than the second, but still they did not sleep. The fourth night came. Their eyes were red and their eyelids felt heavy. A drowsiness came over them that they could not dispel. The woman said, "I will close my eyes just for a moment."

But Talahoyama shook her, saying, "No, not even for a moment."

So they sat there, feeling a great weariness flow into their bodies.

At this moment Gogyeng Sowuti, Spider Grandmother, came into the house. She said, "I will try to help you. Here is pine gum I have brought from the forest. Use it to stick your eyelids open." They put the pine gum on their eyelids. Spider Grandmother said, "Now I am putting something into the fire to make it glow different colors. Watch what you see there. It will help you to stay awake."

After Spider Grandmother had gone, they sat watching the fire change colors, and sometimes they saw pictures in the flames. But just before dawn the woman's head went down and she drifted away into sleep. As she did so the spirit left her body and she died.

Talahoyama was sick with grief. The people buried his wife. Now he was alone. He did not go hunting, he did not work his fields. Instead, he went and sat by his wife's grave. Day after day it went on like this. His friends came to him. They said, "You cannot remain here by your wife's grave forever. Your wife is dead. You are alive. When you are alive, you must go on living."

He replied, "Other things no longer interest me. The only thing I want is to be with my wife."

Every day he went to sit by the grave. And it happened that one day he saw a glow of light from the place where his wife was buried. He found that he could see through the ground just as though it were clear water. He saw his wife. She was sitting there combing her hair.

She spoke to Talahoyama. She asked, "Why do you stay there all the time?"

He answered, "Because I wish to be with you."

She said, "It is useless. You cannot be with me any more. Now I belong to a different world."

He said, "Yes, it is possible. I will come there. I will join you."

His wife spoke sadly. She said, "Four days from now I will leave this grave and go to Moski, the Land of the Dead. For you that is impossible, because your spirit has not been freed from your body. You must stay here and go on living."

But Talahoyama said stubbornly, "Wherever you go, I will follow."

And then he went hunting and killed a deer. He brought meat back to the graveside and said to his wife, "Let us eat together."

She replied, "The kind of food you eat, I can no longer eat it. I can only eat the odor of food."

So Talahoyama made a fire and cooked the meat at the side of the grave. His wife ate the odor of the meat as it cooked. Talahoyama finished eating and he said again, "I will go to Moski with you."

And his wife said again, "No, you cannot enter there."

He said, "You cannot discourage me. I am coming."

His wife replied, saying, "Very well, then, you can try. But you must prepare for the journey. Go home and make four new buckskin shirts for yourself. Make four sets of buckskin leggings and four pairs of moccasins. They will protect you in the cactus fields. Bring some of the baked cornmeal from our house, and bring water. Above all, bring your chiro, the bird cloth that your father made for you when you were small. Before we begin the journey I will tell you the rest. But you must be here early in the morning on the fourth day."

Talahoyama said, "I will be here." He went home and made ready for the journey. He made four sets of buckskin clothing. On the morning of the fourth day he took the baked cornmeal, a jug of water, and his bird cloth. The buckskin clothing he tied in a bundle and carried on his back. He went to his wife's grave. He said, "I am ready."

His wife said, "When I leave I will travel high in the air. It will be hard to see me. Keep your eyes on the eagle feathers in my hair. That way you will not lose sight of me. You will have to run swiftly to keep up. You will come to a great cactus field where the cactuses grow close together. Only your buckskin clothing can protect your skin. When you come to the end of the field your buckskins will be in tatters. Change to new buckskins. In time you will come to another cactus field like the first. When you have passed through it you will have to change your clothes once more. There are four terrible fields like this. After you have passed through the fourth one you will come to a great gorge. Lie down on your bird robe and it will carry you across the gorge. On the other side, you will be in Moski."

Talahoyama said, "I understand. Let us begin."

His wife left the grave and soared swiftly into the air. Even as he watched her, she became small in the distance. He began to run, keeping his eyes on the eagle feathers in her hair. He came to the first cactus field and saw that it was just as his wife had described it. The long needles tore at his clothes, but the buckskin protected his skin. When he came out of the cactus field, his clothes were in tatters. He took them off and put on a new set of buckskins. Soon he came to another cactus field. He passed through it and put on new buckskins. There were two more fields of cactus. After he passed through the fourth field he put on his last remaining buckskins and went on. In time he reached the great gorge. He opened his bird cloth, laid it out on the ground, and lay down upon it. It rose into the air and carried him across the gorge, bringing him to earth on the other side.

Talahoyama could no longer see his wife at all. But now there was a trail before him, and he followed it. Before long he came to where an old man was sitting.

The old man said, "Oh, another one comes."

Talahoyama saw cornfields in the distance. He asked, "Whose fields are these? I do not recognize this place."

The old man answered, "Why, as everyone knows, this place is Moski, the Land of the Dead. These fields belong to the Coyote Clan of Sikyatki."

"Sikyatki?" Talahoyama repeated in wonder. "How can that be? The village of Sikyatki perished long ago and lies in ruins."

The old man said, "Nevertheless, here in Moski the village of Sikyatki still exists."

Talahoyama went further. He saw a man tilling a field, and he asked, "Whose fields are these?"

"These fields belong to the Sand Clan of Awatovi," the man said.

"But there is no village of Awatovi," Talahoyama said. "It was destroyed long ago, and nothing is left of it but stones and broken pots."

The man said, "Here in Moski things are different."

Talahoyama went further and saw another man sitting by the trail. He asked, "You, Uncle, why are you sitting here?"

The man looked up at Talahoyama. He said, "Why, I came here when I died. But I did wicked things in my life and brought misfortune to my village. Therefore, I am allowed to come only a few steps at a time. I walk a little, then I must stop and wait. I have been on my way a long time. I do not know when I will get to the end of the trail."

Talahoyama went on, and next he saw a woman carrying a heavy basket on her back. It was filled with stones, but instead of a forehead strap made of hide she used the string of a hunting bow. It cut into her skin and gave her great pain.

Talahoyama asked, "Why are you using a bowstring instead of a strap?"

She answered, "When I was alive I brought disgrace on my clan. That is why I must carry my basket this way until I arrive where I am going."

Talahoyama hurried on, coming in time to a place where the trail forked to the north and to the west. A two-horn priest was standing there. On his head he wore the horns of a mountain sheep, and sacred eagle feathers hung over his face. The two-horn priest barred the path, saying, "I heard that you were coming. But you cannot go any further. Turn back."

"I cannot go back," Talahoyama said, "for I am following my wife."

"So I have heard," the two-horn priest said. "But Moski is only for the dead."

"I know nothing about such matters," Talahoyama said. "I only know that wherever my wife goes, I will go there also."

"You do not understand the way it is in this place," the two-horn priest said patiently. "Look around you. This is not the land of the living. Only the spirits of the dead are here. You saw those people on the trail back there. They could not come to Moski until their bodies died and were buried. The man who walked a little and rested a little, in the other world he killed a person of his village, and he also insulted the kachinas. Because of him, for a whole year no rain came to his clan's fields, and the crops dried up. Therefore the people starved. It is for this that he suffers now. And the woman who carried the basket of stones with only a bowstring across her forehead, she is punished because she brought disgrace to her clan. Now, this is not the way it is in the land of the living. In that place things are different. Here there are only the spirits of the dead. One who is still alive may not enter."

Talahoyama said, "Yes, I see how things are. Nevertheless I must enter, because my wife is here."

"Well, then," the two-horn priest said, "stay for a while. You will come to understand about matters." He pointed to where the trail divided. He said, "One way, to the north, the trail goes to the Dark Canyon. That is where the evil ones live. There is no light there. It is always night. The other trail, to the west, is for people who have done no evil to others. Where that trail leads there is neither darkness nor sunlight, only a perpetual grayness like the first light of dawn. Go that way."

Talahoyama took the west trail, and the two-horn priest followed him. They came to a large flat field. It looked like the top of the mesa behind Oraibi. There were many young people there. They were having a rabbit hunt, laughing and calling back and forth to one another. The young men would catch the rabbits and bring them to the girls. Talahoyama saw his wife among them, and he ran toward her. When they saw him coming, they cried out, "Look! A living person is there!" They scattered and ran away. Talahoyama's wife ran, too. He ran after her into the village, calling out to her, but she did not stop. He said, "It is I, Talahoyama. Why are you running away?"

She came to a house and went up a ladder. Talahoyama tried

to follow her, but the rungs of the ladder were made of sunflower stalks, and they broke under his weight. He saw his wife up above on one of the rooftops. A man was there. He took the woman's hands, and they went away together. Talahoyama did not see them any more. He stood there silently for a long time looking at the place where they had disappeared.

The two-horn priest said, "You see how it is."

Talahoyama stopped looking at the roof. He turned his eyes to the ground. He said, "Is she not my wife? Why did she run from me?" And after a moment he asked the two-horn priest, "Who is the man who welcomed her?"

The two-horn priest said, "Things are not the same here. She has gone to live with her first husband, the one who died before you married her."

It was then that Talahoyama understood why he could not live in Moski. He said, "I didn't know it would be this way. Now I will return to my own village."

He went back the way he had come. He passed the woman who carried the heavy basket with a bowstring against her forehead, and the man who endlessly walked a little and rested a little. He passed the fields of the Sand Clan of Awatovi and the fields of the Coyote Clan of Sikyatki. When he came to the great gorge he crossed it on his bird cloth. Slowly and carefully he made his way through the four cactus fields. And when he came to the place where he had begun his journey, Gogyeng Sowuti, Spider Grandmother, was waiting for him.

She said, "You have been to Moski and returned. Now you

understand what you did not understand before. The dead must be with the dead. The living must live with the living. When a woman dies and goes to Moski, her husband must remain behind until his turn comes. Nor can a wife go with her husband when he dies. A dead spirit is unwelcome among the living, and a living person is unwelcome among the dead. Each happening in the world has its own time. Only when a person's spirit leaves the dried stalk of his body can he go to Moski. Until then he must live."

"Yes," Talahoyama said, "it is so."

Then Spider Grandmother said, "Because you have been in the Land of the Dead, you must be purified before you go among people. Otherwise you will bring death into the village." She made a fire and put a pot of water over it. It became hot. Talahoyama removed his clothes, and Spider Grandmother poured the water on him. And doing what only she knew how to do, she removed his outer skin and threw it into the fire.

She gave him fresh clothes to wear. "When you return to the village, you must not tell where you have been or what you have seen. Otherwise the people will regard you as a dead spirit. If they ask, 'Where have you been?' tell them, 'I have been hunting.'" Spider Grandmother put red paint on his face, for that was what a man wore when he went out for game. She gave him a hunting bow, and she gave him the carcass of a deer. Then she departed.

Talahoyama put the deer on his shoulder and returned to the

village. The people were surprised, and they welcomed him, for they had believed him to be dead.

He said, "I went hunting. Here is the deer."

He washed his hands, as hunters do, to remove the scent of game.

He entered his house.

He went on living.

Coyote's Needle

❖

Coyote was living there west of Oraibi, and north of Oraibi was the house of the hummingbird. One day Coyote was prowling along the edge of the village where the people left their rubbish. He thought, "Here I will find something useful." The hummingbird saw Coyote there. He saw Coyote pick things up and throw them away. So the hummingbird dug a hole, got into it, and covered himself with dirt, leaving his long narrow bill protruding. Coyote arrived, thinking, "Aha, here is a needle. I have found something." He took hold of the hummingbird's bill and lifted it, pulling the bird out of the ground.

The hummingbird said, "Is this the way that friends do? I was sleeping, and you pulled me out of my kiva."

Coyote was embarrassed. He said, "I regret it. I thought you were a needle. Let us forget the matter. Come to my place this evening, and we will smoke a pipe together." The hummingbird agreed.

In the evening the hummingbird went to visit Coyote. Coyote saw him coming. He dug a hole in the ground, entered it, covered himself with dirt, and left his nose protruding out of the ground. The hummingbird approached. He saw Coyote's nose, saying, "Aha, I have found a jug. I will use it to carry water." He took hold of Coyote's nose and lifted it.

Coyote followed his nose out of the ground. He said, "Is this the way it is with friends? I was sleeping in my kiva, and you pulled me out roughly."

The hummingbird was embarrassed. He said, "I regret it. I thought you were a jug. Let us smoke and forget the matter."

They entered Coyote's house. They smoked together. They forgot the matter.

How the Tewas
Came to First Mesa

❖

The Tewa people were living at a place called Tewageh, near the river now known as the Rio Grande. Many times they had to fight the Kiowas, the Comanches, and the Utes to protect their village, and they were considered to be brave warriors. It is said that sometimes the women fought side by side with the men to defend Tewageh from raiding tribes.

Now, the Hopis also were being attacked. Utes, Paiutes, and Comanches raided their villages. In the village of Walpi the leaders of the Bear Clan and the Snake Clan decided to ask the Tewas to come and help them. So they sent messengers to Tewageh. After a long journey to the east, the messengers arrived at the Rio Grande. When they reached Tewageh, they presented prayer sticks to the village chief and the clan chiefs. They said, "In Walpi we are besieged by Utes, Paiutes, and Comanches. They steal our food, our horses, and our women. You, the Tewa people, are known for your courage. Our people invite you to come and build new homes on our mesa. If you are there the enemy will be discouraged and turn back. Help us to protect our village. In exchange we will give you land for your fields. You will become our brothers."

The Tewa chiefs listened. They said, "We will consider it."

The messengers returned to Walpi. Many days passed. The enemy went on raiding, but the Tewas did not appear. So again messengers were sent to Tewageh with prayer sticks. They inquired whether the Tewas were coming. The Tewas said, "We are considering it." The messengers returned to Walpi and more time passed.

The enemy was pressing hard against Walpi, but still the Tewas did not come. A third time Walpi sent messengers to Tewageh. They asked, "Are our Tewa brothers going to come?"

And the Tewas replied, "You ask our people to leave their homes and fields to go to a strange place. That is not a small thing. Nevertheless, we are considering it."

A season passed, but the Tewas did not come. Finally, messengers were sent from Walpi for the fourth time. They said, "Brothers, we are not strong enough to turn back our enemies. If the Tewas do not come, how shall we survive?"

This time the chief of Tewageh replied, "Yes, we have thought about the matter. Any Tewa warriors who wish to go to your country with their families, they may go." And he had it announced in the village that whoever wanted to leave to fight for the Hopi people in Walpi should make himself ready. First one man and then another said, "I am ready." Those who chose to go stood on one side of the village, and when they numbered half of all the men in Tewageh the chief called out, "No more. Half of our people may go to help Walpi. The other half must remain here. We cannot abandon our village."

Those who were going prepared themselves. There were more than four hundred of them. The men fixed their weapons, and the women packed food for the journey. They went out of Tewageh toward the west. It was a long march. They first came to the place now known as Canoncito. They halted. They made a temporary camp there and rested for some days. Then they continued on to a place called Awpimpaw, meaning Duck Spring, near the present town of Grants. Again they rested for some days, and after that they journeyed as far as Bopaw, meaning Reed Spring, not far from where the town of Ganado is today. They made a temporary camp there and rested. After that they went on, arriving at last at Kwalalata, the Place of the Bubbling Water. That was their fourth stop, and now they built a temporary village on the ridge of the mesa somewhat west of Walpi. Here they waited for final word from the Hopi about where the Tewa would build a permanent village.

So, after so much time, the Tewas had come. But the people of Walpi were no longer certain of them. They had doubts. The Tewas announced their presence, saying, "Brothers, we have arrived." Still the Walpi people did not invite them to come any closer. They said among themselves, "How do we know the Tewas will protect us?" And according to what the old people tell us now, the people of Walpi made contact with the Utes. They invited the Utes to come and attack Walpi. In this way the people of Walpi sought to learn how well the Tewas could fight.

Then the Walpi chief sent a message to the Tewas, informing them that the enemy was coming and warning them to be prepared.

The leader of all the Tewas who had come on the long march from Tewageh was a man named Agayoping. He ordered the men to prepare for battle. They made arrows and repaired their lances, bows, and shields. Agayoping said, "Four times they sent for us. Now that we have come, who knows whether we are welcome? Now they are testing us. They want to know if we have courageous hearts. Very well. Let us meet the enemy."

Agayoping sent scouts to the north. On the third night the scouts saw many campfires in the direction of Black Mountain. On the fourth day they saw the enemy approaching on horseback. They saw flashes of light reflecting from the mirrors worn by the riders and thus knew them to be Utes. They returned to report what they had seen, saying, "Brothers, the warriors that are coming are Utes."

The Tewas painted their faces. Agayoping said, "Let us do what we know how to do well. The Utes, they come in great numbers. There are few of us. The Hopi are not sure of us. They want to know if we are brave. Very well. We are Tewas. To be a Tewa is to have courage. We shall split into two parties. One party will meet the Utes in front. The other will go behind them."

A messenger arrived from Walpi announcing that the enemy were approaching.

Agayoping said, "Yes, we are ready."

The women were told to remain in the village, and some men were assigned to stay with them in case the Utes should reach the ridge. Then the Tewas went down to the gap. They could see the Utes riding along Wepo Wash. They saw them dismount and go down into the wash to plan their attack.

Agayoping said, "Let us begin. One party will approach from the front, the other from the rear. Strike them hard. Shoot first at their war leader, he who gives them counsel. When you have destroyed him, another will take his place. Strike him down from his horse. A war party without a counselor is already half finished."

The Tewas went down. They broke into two parties, one going one way, one another. One party advanced standing up so the Utes could see them. The other went crawling unseen among the rocks. The battle began. The best Tewa bowmen were in front. They rained arrows on the Utes. The Utes charged their horses among the Tewas. Dust rose from the ground and hung like a cloud around the battle. An arrow struck the counselor of the Utes, and he fell from his horse. Another man took his place, but an arrow struck him also. The Utes fell back. They regrouped and charged again. But now the Tewas' second war party attacked from the rear, and the Utes turned aside to avoid being caught in a trap. They retreated to a place now called Tukchu—Meat Point—because it was there that they had hidden their dried meat before the attack. At Tukchu they tried to make a stand, shooting arrows from behind their meat bags. But once again they were caught between two Tewa war parties, and they had to move again. From then on the Utes had no place to hide, and the Tewas drove them through the valley. The Utes signaled to the Tewas to end the fighting, but the Tewas would not stop. At last only three Ute warriors were left. One of them tied a cloth on the end of his bow and waved it.

Agayoping called out to his men to stop the fighting. He went forward alone to speak to the Ute survivors.

One of them spoke, saying, "Who are you people? For we see that you are not Hopi."

Agayoping said, "No, we are Tewas."

The Ute said, "My cousin, we did not know it was you. We thought we were fighting the men of Walpi."

Agayoping said, "No, though you came to make war against Walpi it is we, the Tewas, that you have been fighting. My cousin, why do you try to bring trouble to Walpi? The people there are peaceful. They do not make war on you. Why do you attack them?"

The Ute replied, "We came only to get corn and other supplies."

Agayoping said, "The Utes have made a mistake, as you have discovered. We are not going back to Tewageh. We are going to stay up there on the mesa. If your war parties come again we shall be waiting."

The Ute said, "No, we shall not return. Here is my bow as a token. It is not made of wood, which rots. It is made of elkhorn and lasts forever. I give it to you as a pledge. If my elkhorn bow ever rots, only then shall we meet again."

"Very well," Agayoping said, accepting the bow. "I have heard your pledge. Go back now to your people. Tell them how it was when the Utes met the Tewas."

The three Utes went their way. The Tewas took the scalps of their slain enemies. They looked for the bodies of four of the Utes who had shown great bravery. When they found them, they took the hearts from the bodies, and at a certain place on the way back to Walpi they buried the hearts in a common grave. Agayoping said, "Here the hearts of the brave are buried. Let us see what grows from this spot in time to come." Years later a juniper tree grew out of the grave. It is still there, and the Tewas call the place Pintoy, meaning the Place of Hearts.

The Tewa warriors returned to the gap and found the village chief and the clan chiefs of Walpi waiting for them.

Agayoping said, "It is done. The Utes are dead, all except three who returned to their homes. Many Tewas also died. But now it is finished. Here are the scalps. Take them."

The Walpi people said, "No. Keep the scalps. They are yours. You have been tested. Now your people can come and build their village over there on the north side of the gap."

Agayoping said, "Walpi is south of the gap, but you give us a place north of the gap. How then can we protect you? How would we even know if the enemy came silently in the night? No, if we are to defend Walpi we must sit like a watchdog before your door."

The Walpi chiefs reconsidered the question, and at last they said, "Very well, then. Build your village on the point of land just south of the gap."

Agayoping replied, "You ask us to live on a small piece of earth. That is not enough. Our numbers are few now, but in time we will have more people. We must have room to grow."

So the chiefs of Walpi conferred again, and at last they walked to the place where the Tewa village now stands. They said, "The earth here is yours. Build your village on this spot. Now, look beyond the mesa to the east. There you see Eagle Point. And to the west you see Big Water Point. All the land between them is for your fields. Grow your corn there. And may the Tewa people flourish."

"Very well," the Tewas said. "It is agreed."

Then the Bear Clan chief said, "If a Tewa man needs a wife, let him seek her among the Hopi. If a Hopi man needs a wife, let him come freely to the Tewas to ask for her. This way the bonds between us will grow strong."

But Agayoping replied, "It is too soon to accept such a thing. We do not know if we can live together forever. We came in trust because you sent for us. But when we arrived you let us remain out there on the ridge. You did not trust us. You did not invite us to come closer. Instead, you sent for the Utes. So how can we tell about the future? If something should happen, perhaps you would tell us to leave. If we have children and grandchildren living in Walpi, how could we ever go away and leave them behind? So let us wait. We will see how things go. Later on we can speak of this matter again."

The Walpi chiefs said, "Yes, another time we shall speak of it again. We shall grow closer. We shall share each other's language."

Agayoping answered them, saying, "Since you did not trust us, how then can we share our speech?" He took an ear of corn. He gave it to the Walpi chiefs and asked them to chew the kernels in their mouths. When they had done this, he said, "Put what you have chewed into my hand." They did so. Then he placed the chewed corn in his mouth and swallowed it.

The Walpi people said, "What does it mean that you swallow what we have chewed?"

Agayoping replied, "It means that the language that comes from your mouths, we shall swallow it and make it our own. We, too, shall speak Hopi."

The Walpi chiefs said, "Very well. You chew corn for us, and we shall take it into our own mouths and swallow it."

Agayoping and some of his men began to chew. While they chewed they dug a deep hole in the ground. When it was deep enough they spat the chewed corn into it and covered it with dirt and stamped it down.

The Walpi people asked, "What does it mean?"

Agayoping replied, "It means that what comes from our mouths will never be in the mouths of the Hopis. We cannot share our language with you. It would give you power over us. You would learn the secrets of our kivas. You would say, 'Hopis and Tewas, they are the same thing.' We shall speak Hopi so that we can communicate with you. But the Hopis shall not speak

Tewa." And this is how it came to be that all Tewas speak the Hopi language, but Tewa, the Hopis have never mastered it.

The Tewas built their village. At the center, around the plaza, the Bear Clan built its houses. The Sun Clan built a little beyond, and beyond that the Cloud Clan built. The Corn Clan built its houses facing the eastern approach to the village. Around the edges the other clans built—the Tobacco Clan, the Green Corn Clan, the Parrot Clan, the Cottonwood Clan, the Stick Clan, and the Shell Clan. The people of Walpi called the new settlement Hano, but the Tewas called it Tewa Village.

Agayoping instructed that the record of the battle against the Utes be engraved in stone, and it was done. A picture of a Ute shield was cut into the cliffs near the gap, and next to it were cut many small marks to show how many Utes fell in the fighting.

In time other Tewas came from villages on the Rio Grande to live in the new settlement on First Mesa. They brought with them the sacred masks and other ritual objects that Agayoping's people had left behind in Tewageh. The Tewas lived on, and there they have remained to this day.

Notes on Hopi
Oral Literature

❖

The Hopi people have been living in the neighborhood of their present villages for something like six or seven hundred years. During the preceding ten or twelve centuries, their ancestors, the Anasazi people (a Navaho word meaning "the ancient ones") occupied a large region somewhat to the north in the San Juan basin. One of the main Anasazi culture areas was in the environs of Kayenta, near which these people built the spectacular cave villages now known as Keet Seel, Betatakin, and Inscription House. When these pre-Hopi (or perhaps almost-Hopi) residents of the cave villages abandoned their settlements toward the end of the thirteenth century because of a sustained drought, they moved southward. In time some of them reached the southern edge of Black Mesa, where the Hopi villages of today are standing.

The people did not come all at once. As in still earlier days, each clan (often nothing more than a slightly extended family) followed its own route, its own timetable, and its own counsel, stopping now and then to build temporary homes and to grow new supplies of food. Some migrating groups settled farther to the east, along the Rio Grande River in what is now New Mexico. Some of the clans, it is said, went west, and some went south into what is now called Mexico.

Though the Hopis, their Rio Grande cousins, and their Anasazi ancestors were town builders (hence the name the Spanish gave them—Pueblos, meaning cities), they appear to have been afflicted with a nomadic drive that was never completely satisfied. Their wanderings, some short, some long, have left thousands of square miles of the southwestern terrain dotted with the ruins of ancient villages. The alternate migrations, settlements, and abandonment of settlements are the substance of a considerable part of the Hopi oral literature. Beginning with the creation myths themselves and running throughout the legends and historical accounts, there is a seemingly endless search for something more just, or more satisfying, or more peaceful, or more in balance with nature, or in fulfillment of prophecy. To reach the Upper World from the Lower, the people had to pass through an opening in the sky, and this was a migration in itself. The wanderings of the clans and other groups did not really come to an end until recent times. Some of the clans believe that their preordained migrations have not yet been completed.

While droughts and the arrival of other peoples in the region may have had much to do with the Hopi peregrinations, traditional accounts put heavy stress on religious and moral motivations, as well as on dissension between villages, clans, and individuals. Thus, the destruction of the village of Awatovi by

other Hopi villages was prompted by an alleged moral break-
down among Awatovi's people. (An evident symptom of "moral
failure" was the acceptance into Awatovi of Catholic missionaries.) An attack against the village of Sikyatki that dispersed its
population was the result of a feud with neighboring Walpi.
The abandonment of Lamehva and the migration of its people
to another part of the mesa was caused by a feud with neighboring Kaiotakwi. (See the story "Sikakokuh and the Hunting
Dog.") The people of Payupki left their village and migrated to
Zuñi because they feared the people of Tikuvi. (See the story
"The Foot Racers of Payupki.") According to legend the village
of Pivanhonkapi perished and its few survivors were scattered
because the people lost their moral standards. (See the story
"How the Village of Pivanhonkapi Perished.") Some Hopis say
that the old cave villages near Kayenta were abandoned not
because nature was too hard, but because it was too good. Life
was so easy there, according to the explanation, that the Kayenta people began to forget their religious values and fell into
careless ways. Their chiefs felt that only in the hard life,
symbolized by the stubby blue ear of corn, could the people
remain strong, and so Keet Seel, Betatakin, and Inscription
House were given up in favor of less generous surroundings
elsewhere. The founding in this century of the villages of
Hotevilla (Hotavala) and Bacobi (Bakavi) resulted from dissension in Oraibi. If the reasons given by tradition for the more
remote migrations do not always coincide with the proba-
bilities, the testimony of the oral literature nevertheless makes

clear that motivations other than drought and war were involved.

As with oral traditions everywhere, Hopi myths and legends are continually reshaped in the process of being passed on. A narrator may embellish, or his memory may err, or he may sense an inconsistency and attempt to rationalize it away. Or he may weave later knowledge into ancient accounts. For example, some versions of the emergence myth note that not only Indians and white men came from below into the Upper World, but black men also, even though the Hopis saw their first black man at the time of the Spanish conquest. One informant said in response to a question that the Hopis came to Black Mesa from Mongolia. Another, on being asked about the four worlds of the Hopi, said he believed there were more yet to come, as evidenced by the landing on the moon and the exploration of Mars.

If there is a significant amount of rationalizing the motives of the Hopi restlessness and the causes of great events, it is usually in the direction of seeking moral justifications. As a technology-oriented people we look to science for explanations. As a theology-centered people the Hopis look for answers based on theological principles.

In Hopi tradition, myth, legend, and historical accounts are equally valid records of the tribal experience, and to my knowledge no hard and fast distinction between them is made. Mythological elements are interwoven with events that may have occurred in recent centuries, or even years. Gogyeng Sowuti, Spider Grandmother (literally, Spider Old Woman) appears frequently in stories of recent derivation. In the story "How the Village of Pivanhonkapi Perished," Spider Grandmother intervenes to save Oraibi from the flames. In "The Foot Racers of Payupki," a story that is essentially a historical record, Spider Grandmother intercedes again. In many tales it is the presence and actions of Spider Grandmother that transform what would otherwise be mere incident into story.

Among personalities associated with the emergence who play a continuing role in the oral literature are the brothers Pokanghoya and Polongahoya, demigods often identified as the Warrior Twins. They are credited with turning primeval mud into rock and with exterminating the giants and other monsters who once inhabited the earth. In their role as giant killers they recall the Mayan myth in which two warrior gods (twins) are assigned the task of destroying the earth giants. But the Hopi twins are *enfants terribles* as well as benefactors, and their pranks range from simple mischief to death-dealing acts. Muyingwa, a germination god, is also involved from time to time in the affairs of men.

The Hopis themselves are aware of the existence of numerous variants of their myths, legends, and historical accounts. Even the emergence myth is told differently in different clans and villages. Each clan is regarded as the proprietor of and supreme authority on its own history. Nevertheless, even within a clan the history may vary from one village to another. There are "Oraibi versions," "Walpi versions," and "Shongopovi versions." Some people maintain that the "true versions" of the legends are known only to the priesthood and the members of important kiva societies. But even these "true versions" may differ from one another.

Certain elements and motifs recur frequently in Hopi stories. Foot racing, for example, either for pure sport or as a contest for high stakes, is commonplace as an event on which the outcome of a story hangs. The Hopis traditionally have regarded running as a manly capability, and they tell many tales about the endurance and speed of their men and boys, and sometimes of their women and girls as well. It is said that before the village of Moencopi was built, men who had fields in that place used to run there all the way from Oraibi in the early morning hours, cultivate their corn, and run all the way back to Oraibi in the evening. There may have been shortcuts in those days, but by modern road the distance from Oraibi to Moencopi is more than fifty miles, and it is likely that it required more time than is now remembered. In any case, the Hopis consider their "old-timers" to have been exceptional runners, and the consequences of many tales hinge on that capability, as is seen in two stories included in this collection, "The Boy Who Crossed the Great Water and Returned" and "The Foot Racers of Payupki." Most accounts of the trouble between Walpi and Sikyatki include a kachina race that led directly to the tragic denouement.

Gambling is another motif that occurs frequently. Sometimes it involves commonplace sports such as racing and nahoyda-datsya (a kind of field hockey), sometimes more exotic contests. In the story "Joshokiklay and the Eagle," the protagonist is forced to play totolospi (a kind of dice game using sticks as throwing pieces), and he is saved from death only by another gambling contest won by the kachinas who come to protect him. The crucial event in "The Boy Who Crossed the Great Water and Returned" is the footrace in which the loser is doomed to death. In the Payupki story the stakes of the race are the women of Tikuvi, and in the later shooting contest the stakes are cattle.

Sorcery, magic, and medicine are ubiquitous in the literature. People die and are revived through magic, contests are resolved by sorcery, and supernatural forces are lurking everywhere. People are readily turned into animals and animals into people, but this kind of transformation is not necessarily ominous or evil. It projects something of the Hopi attitude that all living creatures are cousins and that all life is more closely related than outward forms suggest. Miraculous transformations are merely an unusual aspect of the ordinary.

One observation that a reader of these and other Hopi tales will readily make is that everything seems to come in fours. It is always four years, or four days, or four attempts, or four events, or four games, or four directions, or four messengers. The number four is important ritualistically, and it pervades virtually all Hopi narrations.

Most storytelling is done during the winter months, which the Hopis regard as the proper time for such things. It is during this period that at home and in the kivas the older people relate the legends of the villages and the clans and tell stories about persons who have done great things or made miraculous journeys.

There is usually a formalized beginning for tales when they are told in their natural setting. The narrator says, "Aliksai," and if the listeners want him to proceed, they respond, "Oh." The narrator then says something like, "There was a village," or, "The people were living there." A sense of "history" is imparted in this way even to animal tales. Legends or tales involving humans almost invariably are given a locale, whether an existing or an extinct village. Sometimes the narrator will identify the house in which the protagonist lived, much in this fashion: "Long ago there was a family living in Oraibi just north of where the such-and-such kiva is now located." Or, "In the very house where so-and-so now lives, there was a young man." Even myth-legends going back to the period of the migrations have this element of precisely identified places where events are acted out. Names of characters are generally considered to be of secondary importance, and often even a long story is told without mention of personal names.

With the exception of one short humorous tale borrowed from the Voth collection (H. R. Voth, *The Traditions of the Hopi*, 1905), the stories in this book are part of a large body of narrations gathered by the author in 1968 and 1969 from Hopi storytellers in or near the Hopi villages. The principal informants and narrators were members of the Bear, Reed, Tobacco, Rabbit, and Coyote Clans living in Walpi, Moencopi, Hano (Tewa), and Shongopovi. It was my wish and intention to identify the various narrators of these tales and legends and to acknowledge their specific contributions to this collection. However, for a number of reasons having to do with personal relations within the Hopi community, most of the narrators preferred not to be named. Under such circumstances I am obliged to omit the customary acknowledgments. But to all those Hopi men and women who were so understanding and generous in their help and who through these tales and legends have given the rest of us an opportunity to perceive something of Hopi values and traditions, I give my thanks.

Notes on the Stories

❖

How the People Came from the Lower World

Among the innumerable variants of the emergence myth, there are a good many unreconciled differences. Mostly they are differences resulting from individual embellishment, ex post facto rationalizing, or emphasis on the traditions and experiences of a particular clan. The Parrot Clan has one record of events, the Bluebird Clan another, the Reed Clan a third, and so on. In some renditions of the emergence story, there is no mention of the Fire Clan, but the Bear Clan version speaks of the Fire Clan in explaining how the Bear Clan came to be the first in rank. According to this version the first person to climb from the Lower World to the Upper World belonged to the group—that is, an extended family—that was eventually to be known as the Fire Clan. Because this man emerged first, the Hopis offered him the chieftainship and asked him to lead them. But he asked to be excused on the grounds that the responsibility was too great. So

160

the leader of the group that was to become the Bear Clan accepted the responsibility, and it is for this reason that the Bear Clan holds the first rank among the Hopis today. (All the villages except one have Bear Clan members as their chiefs.)

The account given in this story of how the clans received their names is considerably abbreviated. Numerous clans are said to have taken their names at the camping place near the dead bear. Here is the scene as depicted by one informant:

"When the people first started out, they didn't have any clans. That is, they were not known by certain clan names. When they were wandering through the country, they came to a dead bear. Some people looked at it and said, 'That bear hasn't been dead very long.' They said, 'Since we're one group of people, why can't we claim to be Bear Clan members? Let's call ourselves the Bear Clan.' They said, 'All right. That's the way we'll distinguish ourselves in case we meet other people. We'll tell them we're Bear Clan.' They said, 'The bear is close to that spruce. While we're here, who wants to become a Spruce Clan?' Someone said, 'I will with my brothers. We'll become Spruce Clan.' They separated themselves to become Spruce Clan. After the people skinned the bear, they began to make straps out of the hide. Years ago they used to use wide straps to carry their bundles. They called that pikoysa. Someone said while making it, 'Say, I want to become Pikoysa Clan.' People said, 'All right. If you distinguish yourself as Pikoysa Clan, go that way.' After they stayed there for a while, bluebirds came down to pick on the bear's fat. One fellow said, 'Say, that's a pretty bird there. I want to become Bluebird Clan.' The people said, 'All right. You want to be Bluebird Clan. Separate yourselves from the others as Bluebird Clan.' The carcass was still there, and after a while some fellow looked inside and saw it was fat. He said, 'Say, it's all so greasy. I better belong to the Grease Cavity Clan.' It's called Wikoshuwoma. While they were staying there, an old gopher made its mound right under the carcass. Somebody saw it and said, 'That's a gopher. I want to be Gopher Clan.' So there are your affiliations—your Bear, your Spruce, your Strap, your Bluebird, and your Gopher."

Most generally the creation of the land, the mountains, the sun, the moon, the animals, and man is attributed to the deity Huruing Wuhti. But after the period of initial creation, one hears mostly of Spider Grandmother creating things and assisting the human race. A knowledgeable informant stated that these two deities are in fact one, and are regarded as creator and provider:

"Huruing Wuhti is the same as Mother (Grandmother) Spider. She is called Huruing Wuhti because she is in possession of everything like corals and shells and hard things. Gogyeng Sowuti, Spider Grandmother, is also called Huruing Wuhti. There are two names for her. She is really Mother Earth. They call her Spider Grandmother because the spider makes a hole in the ground and lives in the earth. They use different names to distinguish the direction. Gogyeng Sowuti, that name refers to the direction of the rising sun. Huruing Wuhti, that name refers to the west. But it's really Mother Earth they're talking about—

the spirit of female fertility. Whatever is planted, Mother Earth takes care of it."

It is possible to speculate that somewhat different creation accounts, one featuring Huruing Wuhti and another Gogyeng Sowuti, were contributed by different peoples merging into the Hopi culture. While the blending process was largely successful, it has left some contradictions unresolved. For the Hopis, however, the pieces all seem to fit together—even though in some stories it is not Spider Grandmother or Huruing Wuhti who creates the spectacular features of the earthly scene, but the Warrior Twins, Pokanghoya and Polongahoya. Sometimes the deity Masauwu is credited with these creations. And sometimes, as in this version, the medicine men play a role.

The deity Masauwu is described here as Lord of the Upper World and Guardian of the Land of the Dead. It is apparent from conversations with Hopis that they have difficulty in conveying in English the exact nature of this deity. The word masauwu is used in other contexts as meaning "a dead spirit" or "the spirit of a person who has died." The investigator H. R. Voth, who studied the Hopis three-quarters of a century ago, consistently translated the word masauwu into "skeleton," which is patently misleading in reference to a dead spirit or to the deity. "Death" or "Deity of Death" may be as close as we can come in English to the Hopi meaning of the deity's name. In some renditions, when Masauwu is first seen by the Hopis, he is wearing a kindly face. In others he is described as having hideous and frightening features. The contradiction seems to be resolved in a variant that says the Hopis first see Masauwu sitting before his house, his mask suspended on a pole next to him. His face is friendly though sad, while the mask is terrifying. One is tempted to read into this image what I never elicited from informants—that the appearance of death is frightening, though death itself is benign. Some students of Hopi culture believe that in addition to his other attributes Masauwu is also a deity of germination.

Some variants of the emergence myth say that the opening in the sky above the Lower World was always there, so that when the bird messengers are sent to explore the Upper World, they merely have to pass through it. Others say that the sky was closed and that it had to be pierced by the bamboo planted by the chipmunk.

There is also a lack of consistency about where the souls (the "breath," as the Hopis say) of the dead reside. There is an implicit promise in this story that when a person dies, his soul will return to the Lower World. Nevertheless, Hopis generally concede that souls or spirits of the dead go to Moski, the Land of the Dead, where virtue is rewarded and evil is punished. (See the story "The Journey to the Land of the Dead.")

The version of the emergence myth given here is based on material contributed by several informants.

Coyote Helps Decorate the Night

Coyote usually appears in Hopi tales as a simple trickster and is characterized as greedy, grasping, and gullible. On occasion, as in the lore of other American Indian peoples, he has the characteristics of a culture hero, playing a part in the creation of things. Here he is credited with putting the stars into the sky, though inadvertently. Since his feat clearly conflicts with a mythology that attributes creation of earthly and heavenly features to the deities and demigods, this tale is told lightly, with tongue in cheek, and he remains a kind of comic relief in a literature that is predominantly solemn.

Sikakokuh and the Hunting Dog

While most of the Hopi clans claim that their origins were in far-off places, this story declares that the Reed Clan people were created only a few miles from the villages where they now live. The village of Lamehva, brought to life by Spider Grandmother, was located on the edge of Second Mesa (the second of three southern projections of Black Mesa), and the spring from which it took its name is still there and flowing. The ruins of neighboring Kaiotakwi, near the Burnt Corn rocks, also are still there, the site now being used as a burial place. The stone foundations of Koechapteka, to which the people went after leaving Lamehva, are still visible on a lower ledge of First Mesa, within sight of Walpi. Thus the migration seems to have been a fairly short one, less than a dozen miles by the most direct route. According to most accounts Walpi already existed as a village when the Reed people moved there from Koechapteka, having been settled by other clans that had come from the legendary village of Palatkwapi in the south.

The Beetle's Hairpiece

This brief tale is a comment on vanity, and states implicitly that every creature (person) should accept his own attributes. There is particular comedy for the Hopi listener in the beetle's identification of the kachina dances, which could not possibly occur on the same occasion. When the beetle goes to the top of his house to make his prophetic pronouncement, he is emulating the Crier Chief of the village, and this is an additional source of amusement. His description of his struggle to get off the floor as "the Beetle Dance" recalls an incident involving Anansi, the Ashanti spider trickster. Anansi steals beans from a pot during funeral rites for his mother-in-law. Not wishing to be seen eating, he puts the beans in his hat. When the beans begin to burn his head, he becomes agitated and pushes his hat from one side to the other, declaring that he is doing the Hat-Shaking Dance.

Joshokiklay and the Eagle

The hole in the sky that leads from the ordinary world of people into Tokpela (Endless Space) is a standard feature of Hopi cosmology. It is through a hole such as this one that the people come from the Lower World to the Upper World. There is a temptation to believe that this story actually starts in the Lower World and that the sky opening (sipapu or sipapuni) through which the eagle carries Joshokiklay is the same one that figures in the emergence. If this is not the case and if the story begins in the Fourth or Upper World, then of course one must accept still a Fifth world, which is not consistent with Hopi mythology. The name Tokpela is also given in some accounts to the very first Hopi world, which existed long before the emergence, which further complicates the matter. Nevertheless, informants believe that the events depicted here begin in the modern world and should be accepted as happenings that have no bearing on the basic cosmography.

The concept of the opening overhead is reflected in the construction of most kivas. To enter the kiva from ground level, one goes through the opening and descends to the first level, then continues down to the main chamber on the lower level. In most, if not all, kivas, there is a representation of the emergence sipapu somewhere on the bottom.

Hopi tales and legends abound with examples of miniature magical objects that function just as though they were large. Thus, one grain of corn satisfies Joshokiklay's hunger up on the rock pinnacle, and one drop of water quenches his thirst. A tiny bird carries him to safety on its back. Joshokiklay enters Spider Grandmother's house, or kiva, through a hole only large enough to admit a spider. Spider Grandmother keeps him from freezing in the gambler's kiva by placing a tiny turkey feather on him. And she carries him down to his own world from Tokpela while suspended on a thin thread.

The contest in which the kachinas grow corn, squash, and melons on the floor of the kiva is fanciful only in degree. During the days immediately preceding the Bean Dance, beans are actually sprouted and grown to a height of several inches on the kiva floors, with constantly fueled fires providing the necessary warmth. While the plants do not actually mature, they are symbolic of the powers of the kachinas.

Hasokata, the Gambler, is a character who appears frequently in Hopi tales.

Though Joshokiklay loves his eagles, they are not precisely pets. Traditionally, young eagles are captured and raised to maturity on rooftops, as depicted in this story. They are treated well, but immediately after the Niman festivities in midsummer (signifying the departure of the kachinas from the villages), they are killed and their feathers are kept for ritual use. Properly speaking, it is an eagle sacrifice. The tradition was explained by one informant this way:

"It is a story that the white men don't believe. When we (i.e., the ancestral Hopis during the migrations) went through here they left (lost?) some of the children, who turned into eagles. That's why the Hopis treat them just like babies. When they are going to go after eagles, they make those cradleboards. They get the eagles when they are small. They usually let someone down (from a cliff ledge) tied to a rope. They catch the eagles and put them in the cradleboards. They bring them in just like that. Then they wash the eagles' heads, just like humans. They give them names and put them on top of their houses. Then they feed them. You're not supposed to just feed them any kind of meat.

You're supposed to give them rabbit, fresh meat. When they grow up, about that time there is the Home Dance (Niman festival). The kachinas bring the children dolls or bows and arrows, and they give the eagles that (special) doll, the flat one. So when the dance is over, the next day they wash the eagles' hair again. Then they kill them and remove the feathers. They keep the feathers to make prayer sticks and things like that. They bury the eagles just like humans, and they put flowers on the graves.

"We don't just go out and get eagles from any place. We've got to go where it's ours, belongs to our clan. All this, way clear up to Lee's Ferry, that belongs to the Bear Clan. And then this (other) way, it belongs to the Kachina Clan. My father's people, they have a place over there where they get eagles north of Red Lake. This way (over here) it's ours (Bamboo Clan), down this ridge clear back about fifteen miles. It's about May when they go out to catch the eagles. The Home Dances are in July."

The sequence of events as given here follows the narrator's account except for one brief scene. The narrator's version omitted the descent from Tokpela to Joshokiklay's world by means of the spider's thread. That something was missing was evident to the narrator, who said, "That's the way the story is—he's way up there, now he's down here again." The missing sequence was supplied from a version taken by Voth, "Chorzhukiqolo and the Eagles," which is included in *The Traditions of the Hopi*. Details in the two versions vary considerably.

Mockingbird Gives Out the Calls

The tradition that Yaalpa, the mockingbird, gave the people their languages as they emerged from the Lower World does not inhibit the Hopis from suggesting humorously in this story that he talks too much. The story also takes note of the almost identical appearance of the mockingbird and the catbird and accounts for the fact that while the former is garrulous, the latter says practically nothing.

The Boy Who Crossed the Great Water and Returned

This story contains a rich mixture of familiar elements out of which Hopi narrative is created—a difficult mission undertaken by a heroic figure; a concerned relationship between father and son; certain unexplained mysteries (such as the magic arrows that open the path across the ocean); medicine and sorcery; mystic vision (the father's perception of what the boy must know to cope with the dangers of the journey); the relationships between men and animals (the chief's messengers); and the easy transformation from human form to animal form and back again. And we also see here the athletic contest with life-or-death stakes. Dayveh's journey to the strange land across the sea has the qualities of a miniature Odyssey. As heard in the kivas during the winter storytelling months, the story may well include details or episodes not included in this rendition.

The ball game (nahoydadatsya) that takes place in the plaza of the overseas village is a Hopi form of field hockey, related to games played by other Indians in the Southwest and in Central America. The ball is first covered with sand, and one player from each side takes his turn at trying to uncover it by striking at it with his stick. When the ball is dislodged, the other players join in. The object is to move it across a goal line. In the game described in the story, the girls win because (the narrator explained) they have tucked up their skirts and the boys are distracted by the sight of their legs.

Coyote and the Crying Song

In some of the variants of this Coyote tale, it is a turtle or grasshopper, rather than a dove, that does the crying. In the turtle version the denouement is somewhat different. The turtle (a young one who cries because he is lost) is captured, and Coyote is about to destroy him. He persuades Coyote to throw him into the water. Then he surfaces and, like Brother Rabbit in the briars, calls out, "Don't you know this is my home?" Most, though, not all, of the versions conclude with Coyote's destruction. Here the episode ends with a wry revelation. The crying sounds made by the dove are of course an approximation of its normal call.

Honwyma and the Bear Fathers of Tokoanave

The Bear People of Tokaoanave (Navaho Mountain) are not kachinas or sorcerers but a society possessing great knowledge of curative medicine. There is of course the element of changing into bears and back again to human form, but it is not "magic" in the ordinary sense. Rather, it is an attribute of the society and, in a larger sense, another statement of the Hopi belief in the closeness of all forms of living creatures. In various stories there are comparable groups of Antelope People, Dog People (see "Sikakokuh and the Hunting Dog"), and so on. This intimacy between animal and human forms is reflected also in a traditional assertion that eagles are descendants of human children lost in the wilderness during the early migrations.

In Honwyma's departure to Tokoanave after he dies (just as the dog, Spotted-in-Back, returns to Suchaptakwi in the story "Sikakokuh and the Hunting Dog"), we see a variation on the presumption that after death people go to Moski, the Land of the Dead, or, as the emergence myth suggests, back to the Lower World. The men of Tokoanave are Honwyma's ceremonial fathers because, as an informant explained, "They say that if anybody teaches you to be a medicine man, he becomes your father."

The owa cloth or robe (sometimes called mochapu) is a kind of large shawl woven for girls and is usually translated as "bridal robe." The robes come in sets of two. An act of curative medicine or magic is usually performed under such a cloth. In the emergence story the birds who are to seek out the opening in the sky are created under an owa.

The name Honwyma translates into English as Walks-Like-a-Bear.

Two Friends, Coyote and Bull Snake, Exchange Visits

This is a widespread folklore theme, closely paralleled in an African (Yoruba) tale featuring the tortoise as the trickster. (See "How Ijapa, Who Was Short, Became Long" in Courlander, *Olode the Hunter*.) There are many comparable stories involving an exchange of visits between animal friends that feature some other trick as repayment for bad hospitality.

The Foot Racers of Payupki

Payupki is now an extinct village site on Second Mesa somewhat north of the existing village of Shipaulovi. In some accounts it is said to have been settled not by Hopis but by a group of eastern Pueblos who had left their Rio Grande homes to escape from the overlordship of the Spanish. Later, according to oral tradition, the Payupki people returned to their Rio Grande homeland. This tale specifies that they went to Sioki, placing them among the Zuñis. As noted elsewhere, history is intertwined with supernatural events, and Spider Grandmother's intervention is an important element in the escape to Sioki. Tikuvi, the second Hopi village figuring in the story, also is now an extinct site. Two familiar motifs appear again—foot racing and gambling, both of them crucial to the story line.

❖ ❖ ❖

Why the Salt Is Far Away

Here, as in the story "Sikakokuh and the Hunting Dog," one gets a glimpse of the more innocent side of the character of Pokanghoya and Polongahoya, though it is not clear that they are not being a little mischievous about the grass dance. In the scene where they steal the coiled basketry trays, however, they are characteristically "ornery," as one Hopi described them. The last part of the tale relates them to their role as culture heroes who helped in the creation of things.

How the Village of Pivanhonkapi Perished

One thing that attracts special attention in this story is the theme of punishment meted out to Hopi villages that debase the moral values and become licentious and corrupt. Awatovi was destroyed, according to tradition, for these reasons (plus its acceptance of Catholic missionaries). The legendary town of Palatkwapi somewhere in the south was also destroyed by supernatural events (in some accounts) that developed out of corruption. In the case of Pivanhonkapi the destruction of the village was arranged by its own chief, as also happened, some stories say, in Awatovi. So similar are some of the stories relating to the destruction of various villages, in particular the connivance of their own chiefs, that it is easy to speculate that one such story has provided a literary pattern for others. But H. R. Voth quotes a Shipaulovi informant as saying: "This is the way chiefs often punished their children (people) when they became 'bewitched.' That is one reason why there are so very many ruins all over the country. Many people were killed in that way because their chiefs became angry and invited some chief or inhabitant from other villages to destroy their people."

The Yayaponcha (variously called Yayaponchatu, Yaponcha, Yaya, and Yayatu) are generally known among the Hopis as a group or secret society with special powers. Some Hopis call them simply sorcerers. There are contradicting accounts of their origins. One explanation is that they had their own villages and were not really Hopis. Another is that they were Hopis and that they lived within the existing First Mesa villages, where they frequently put on exhibitions of their magical prowess. One such display was to throw a man down into their kiva, which normally would have been fatal to the victim. But the victim always emerged from the kiva unhurt. One informant spoke of the Yayaponchas calling a scarecrow to come to the top of the mesa from the fields down below. According to the description of the event, the scarecrow did what he was bidden to do. Another story says that one of the Yayaponchas inscribed a mark on a distant mountain by moving his finger in the air. The Yayaponchas have not been active for some years now, but their ritual objects are said to be sealed up in a certain cave on First Mesa.

The village of Huckovi was located, according to the description given in this account, somewhere near Oraibi and presumably on Third Mesa. But Walpi people insist that Huckovi was on a lower ledge of First Mesa, and point out the ruins. It is conceivable that there were two village sites having the same name.

The Sun Callers

Coyote is again cast in his role as dupe, though his stupidity is slightly mitigated by the fact that the rooster is convinced that it is his crowing which causes the sun to rise.

The Journey to the Land of the Dead

This story was identified by the narrator as belonging to the village of Oraibi. The investigator H. R. Voth found two variants of the tale, one in Oraibi and one in the Second Mesa village of Shipaulovi, both of them quite different from this one in dramatic motivation and in the events depicted. But all of the variants share the view of Moski seen here, an inferno conceived by a Hopi Dante. In more extended form, the story goes into great detail about the punishments and sufferings of those who led wicked lives. With nothing more than internal evidence to go on, it is difficult to suggest that this scene may not be Hopi in concept and origin. But it is equally difficult not to wonder whether Christian concepts brought by the Spanish missionaries have been interwoven with purely indigenous motifs.

❖ ❖ ❖

Coyote's Needle

This whimsical anecdote is rewritten, and slightly abbreviated, from a text taken down by Voth. The original appears in his *The Traditions of the Hopi*.

How the Tewas Came to First Mesa

The Tewas occupy one of three villages clustered at the southern tip of First Mesa. To get into either of the other two villages— Sichomovi and Walpi—one must first pass through the Tewa settlement, as indicated in this story. The Hopis call the Tewa settlement Hano, which the Tewas say is a corruption of Tano. The Tewas themselves prefer the name Tewa Village.

This story was told by a Tewa, though some additional details were provided by a Hopi from Walpi. It is of course a Tewa version of history, and is quite different in some respects from the Hopi version. The Hopis say that the Tewas had fled from their Rio Grande homes to get away from the Spanish, and appealed for permission to settle near Walpi. In exchange for a village site and farmlands, the Hopis say, the Tewas undertook the military protection of the First Mesa villages. In regard to the battle against the Utes, the accounts generally agree. The story is more nearly history, as we use that word, than the other tales in this collection. It is disengaged from supernatural events, and there are no mystical or magical explanations.

Hano, or Tewa Village, is the only eastern Pueblo settlement surviving on Hopi land. To the outsider there is little to distinguish it from the Hopi villages. The Tewas have intermarried with the Hopis (despite the original caution of the first settlers), their clans and fraternal groups are intertwined, they share kachinas and dances with the Hopis and they observe the Hopi holidays. But the Tewas continue to speak their own language, and they insist that the secret rituals that take place in their kivas are the ones they brought from their Rio Grande homeland. As for the battle against the Utes, on which so much turned, the Tewas still are in possession of their trophies of war, and the mnemonic record carved in the cliffs is readily visible to anyone going to the mesa top by the main road.

Pronunciation Guide
and Glossary

❖

Numerous Hopi words are pronounced somewhat differently in the various villages. This is well recognized by the Hopis themselves, who frequently refer to the "inaccurate" manner of speech in villages other than their own. The pronunciations given here are those recorded in the narrations.

AGAYOPING (ah-GUY-oh-ping)—the chief of the Tewa expedition to First Mesa

APACHE (uh-PATCH-ee, uh-PAH-chee)—an Indian tribe of the Southwest

AWATOVI (ah-WAH-toh-vee)—an extinct Hopi village near the present settlement of Keams Canyon

AWPIMPAW (aw-PIM-paw)—one of the camping sites of the Tewa expedition

BOPAW (BOH-paw)—one of the camping sites of the Tewa expedition

CASTILLA (kah-STEEL-ha, from the Spanish)—Spaniard

COMANCHE (ko-MAN-chee)—a Southwestern Indian group, or its language (sometimes specified as Shoshone-Comanche)

DAYVEH (DAY-veh)—a boy's name

GOGYENG SOWUTI (GO-gyeng soh-WOO-tee, or soh-WÖ-tee)—Spider Grandmother (literally, Spider Old Woman), one of the main demigods or culture heroes of Hopi tradition

HANO (HAH-noh)—a Tewa village on First Mesa

HA'U (HAH-oo)—a greeting

HASOKATA (hah-SOH-kah-tah)—Gambler, the old man who gambles with people for their lives

HOMOLOVI (hoh-MOH-loh-vee)—a now extinct village near the present town of Winslow

HONWYMA (hon-WYE-mah)—a boy's name, literally, "Walks-with-the-Bears"

HOPI (HOH-pee)—name of the Indians who settled in the region of Black Mesa, sometimes referred to as the western Pueblos

HUCKOVI (HÖ-koh-vee)—an extinct village on Third Mesa, according to the story. Another extinct Huckovi lies at the base of First Mesa.

JOSHOKIKLAY (joh-shoh-KEE-klay)—a boy's name

KACHINA (kah-CHEE-nah)—a benevolent spirit, in the belief of the Hopis and other Pueblo peoples. In ancient times, it is said, the kachinas came in person to the villages at certain times of the year, but now they no longer come, and the kachinas are impersonated by men wearing kachina costumes. There are said to be several hundred different kinds of kachinas. In the kachina ceremonies, the dancers are not prayed to. It is they, on the contrary, who invoke nature on behalf of the people of the villages.

KAIOTAKWI (kye-OH-tah-kwee)—a now extinct village on Second Mesa

KAWAWATAMUY (kah-WAH-wah-tah-MUY)—approximate translation, "Come in, you are welcome."

KIAVAKOVI (kee-AH-vah-koh-vee)—"Someone is coming."

KILT —the knee-length, skirt-like lower garment worn by Hopi men. Its bears no relationship to the Scottish kilt, but there is no other word to properly describe it.

KIOWA (KYE-oh-wah)—a western plains tribe

KIVA (KEE-vah)—an underground meeting chamber, entered by a ladder from the top, used for ritual and ceremonial gatherings

KOECHAPTEKA (kö-CHAHP-teh-kah)—the name of an early village settlement on First Mesa

KWAKWI (KWAH-kwee)—a kind of grass

KWALALATA (kwah-LAH-lah-tah)—one of the camping sites of the Tewa expedition

LALAKON (LAH-lah-kohn)—a women's basket dance

LAMEHVA (lah-MEH-vah)—a now extinct village on Second Mesa. Also the name of the spring, which is still there, from which the village took its name.

MASAUWU (MAH-sah-oo)—deity of Death and Germination, and in some accounts the creator of the Upper World

MASIPA (mah-SEE-pah)—an extinct village on Second Mesa, said to be the first settlement made by the Hopis following the legendary migrations

MISHONGNOVI (mih-SHONG-noh-vee)—a village on Second Mesa

MOENCOPI (MOON-kah-pee)—the westernmost contemporary Hopi village, near Tuba City

MOSKI (MAHS-kee, sometimes MUSS-kee)—the land of the dead

NAHOYDADATSYA (nah-HOY-dah-dahts-yah)—a Hopi ball and stick game somewhat similar to field hockey

NAVAHO (NAH-vah-ho)—the largest southwestern Indian tribe, now a neighbor of the Hopis, but a late intruder into this area

OJAIVI (oh-JYE-vee)—the place on Black Mesa where Masauwu, Lord of the Upper World, resided

ORAIBI (oh-RYE-bee)—a village on Third Mesa, said to be the oldest of the continuously inhabited Hopi settlements

OWA (OH-wah or OH-vah)—the shawl given to girls, generally translated as "bridal robe." It is used in various healing ceremonies.

PAIUTE (PYE-ute)—a southwestern Indian tribe

PAYUPKI (pye-YUP-kee)—a now extinct village on Second Mesa, said to have been settled by eastern Pueblos

PIKI (PEE-kee)—a paper-thin bread, made in sheets and then rolled. A traditional Hopi food.

PIÑON (PEEN-yon)—a variety of pine that produces edible seeds

PINTOY (PIN-toy)—a place associated with the battle against the Utes. A Tewa name signifying "The Place of Hearts."

PIVANHONKAPI (pee-VAHN-hon-kah-pee)—a former village on Third Mesa, north or northwest of Oraibi

PLAZA (from the Spanish, pronounced as in English)—the main courtyard of a village, often near the kiva or kivas, where public gatherings take place, particularly when the kachina dances are held

POKANGHOYA (poh-KAHNG-hoy-ah or poh-GAHNG-hoy-ah)—one of the so-called Warrior Twins, demigods and *enfants terribles* of Hopi mythology. On occasion the twins collectively are called Pokangs.

POLACCA (poh-LAH-kah)—a Hopi village at the foot of First Mesa

POLONGAHOYA (poh-LONG-ah-hoy-ah, also poh-LENG-ah-hoy-ah)—one of the so-called Warrior Twins, demigods and *enfants terribles* of Hopi mythology

SHIPAULOVI (shih-PAWL-oh-vee)—a village on Second Mesa

SHONGOPOVI (shong-OH-poh-vee or shim-OH-poh-vee)—a village on Second Mesa

SICHOMOVI (see-CHOHM-oh-vee)—a village on First Mesa

SIKAKOKUH (see-KAH-koh-kuh)—a boy's name

SIKYATKI (sihk-YAHT-kee)—an extinct village somewhat east of Walpi

SIOKI (see-OH-kee or tsee-OH-kee)—a location in Zuñi country

SIOUX (SOO)—Dakota Indians, or Indians belonging to the Sioux Confederation

SOWITUIKA (soh-WEET-wee-kah)—a former village somewhere in the vicinity of Flagstaff

SUCHAPTAKWI (soo-CHAHP-tah-kwee)—the village to which Sikakokuh journeyed to get his dog

SUPAI (SOO-pye)—also known as Havasupai. An Indian tribe of the Southwest, at present living on a small reservation near the Colorado River.

TALAHOYAMA (tah-LAH-hoy-eh-mah)—a boy's name

TEWA (TAY-wah)—an eastern Pueblo people, some of whom migrated west to Hopi country. The Tewas of First Mesa speak Hopi and are integrated into the Hopi way of life, but they still consider themselves a distinct people.

TEWAGEH (teh-WAH-geh)—the village in what is now New Mexico from which the Tewas migrated to First Mesa

TIKUVI (tih-KOO-vee or tsi-KOO-vee)—an extinct Hopi village

TINTOPAKO-KOSHI (TIN-toh-PAH-koh koh-zhee, zh pronounced like French j)—the name of the dog in the Reed Clan myth. Literally translated, "Spotted Behind."

TOKOANAVE (toh-KOH-ah-nah-veh)—Navaho Mountain, held sacred by the Hopis

TOKPELA (TOHK-pel-lah or DOHK-bel-lah)—"Endless space." The term is also used to denote the First World in Hopi mythology.

TOREVA (toh-RAY-vah)—a well-known spring on Second Mesa

TOTOLOSPI (toh-TOH-lohs-pee, sometimes shortened to toh-TOH-lohs)—a stick-throwing game for gambling

TUKCHU (TOOK-choo, oo as in room)—"Meat Point," a site connected with the battle against the Utes

UTE (YOOT)—the name of a southwestern tribe

WALPI (WAHL-pee)—a village on First Mesa

WEPO (WEE-poh)—the name of a wash passing near First Mesa. In the Southwest, the term wash is used to describe the deeply eroded water runoff channels or gullies that meander among the buttes and mesas. At times of melting snow or heavy rains, they carry water, but most of the year they are dry.

YAALPA (YAH-ahl-pah or YAHL-pah)—mockingbird

YAYAPONCHA (YAH-yah-pon-chah)—the name of a sorcerer's society, or members of that society

ZUÑI (zoo-nyee)—an eastern Pueblo people